CONVICTED OF LOVE

by

Josephine Templeton

WHISKEY CREEK PRESS

www.whiskeycreekpress.com

Published by
WHISKEY CREEK PRESS

Whiskey Creek Press
PO Box 51052
Casper, WY 82605-1052
www.whiskeycreekpress.com

ISBN 978-1-59374-731-2

Credits
Editor: Melanie Billings

Printed in the United States of America

WHAT THEY ARE SAYING ABOUT
CONVICTED OF LOVE

"…absolutely charming. It sparkles with emotion and wit. The story and the characters are all vibrant with life… The dialogue is a rare treat for a historical. It snapped between the characters, sizzling and landing with perfect aim. I will definitely be looking for more work by Josephine Templeton."

~~Reviewed by Ash Arceneaux of Rite of Romance

Dedication

I have to first thank God for giving me the gift of writing, and then my husband, Michael, my inspiration. To my sons, my parents, my sisters (especially Joan) and brothers for putting up with me and my scribbling for all these years. And last, but not least, to my friend Laura Boudle, for letting me pester her about reading the next chapter and telling me what she thinks. Hurry up, Laura, read, read, read!

PART 1

CAMILLE

Chapter 1

End of May 1889
French Quarter
New Orleans, Louisiana

Camille du Carte glared at her aunt's back. The debutante stuck out her lower lip as she tried to figure a way to get the ruby earrings. They were perfect for the dress she planned on wearing to Maggie Lafitte's coming out party. She had to have them.

"Aunt Marie, please," Camille whispered, tears springing readily to her eyes.

The elder woman's spine stiffened as she heard her niece's pitiful tone. Shaking her head, Marie Leonhardt turned around. "Your father gave you a certain amount of money, ma chéri, and you have already reached it."

"But—"

"Camille," Aunt Marie warned, her brown eyes narrowing dangerously.

Camille huffed and stamped her foot. "Fine, then I am going home."

She whirled around and hurried out of the jewelry store. Her aunt's words forbidding her to leave un-chaperoned fell on stone ears. She was too put off with her aunt to stay in her presence one more second.

Blinded by irrational anger, Camille raced down Bienville Street. When she reached the corner of Bourbon Street, she stopped, realizing she had made a mistake. In order to get to her home in the Garden District, she should have stayed on Royal Street. Only then did it occur to her how long a walk she would have. As Camille turned to retrace her steps, a group of drunken sailors tumbled out of a nearby bar, directly in her path. She stopped abruptly, startled by the threat before her.

All four men quit laughing as they took in the young woman before them. Her dark black hair had fallen free of the hairpins and hung in wild array down her back. Her cheeks were rosy red, and her gray eyes flashed like lightening. She was obviously in a temper but that did nothing to stop the advance of the men.

Before the head of the little group had a chance to speak, Camille gathered up her skirts and turned to hightail it in the opposite direction. She ran right into the arms of another sailor. Stunned, she looked up into his eyes with her mouth wide open.

The man smiled, revealing even, white teeth. "Whoa, girl," he said, grabbing her shoulders.

As he watched, the color of her eyes swirled from light gray to dark, reminding him of storm clouds on the verge of turning violent.

"Unhand me, sir," she growled through clenched teeth.

He quickly let go, holding his hands high in the air. "My apologies," he whispered, dipping his head slightly. He looked past her at the lingering sailors. Then, after glancing at the sun's position, he asked of them, "Do you not have someplace else to be?"

Suddenly, the whole lot became embarrassed, and after several "aye, aye, sirs," they took their leave.

Her heart beating rapidly, Camille stood rooted to the spot, intrigued by the color of the stranger's eyes. At first, she would have sworn they were blue, but on closer inspection, she noted that streaks of violet intermingled with the blue. The next second, she realized his attention was back on her, and her cheeks burned with the thought that he had caught her staring.

"You should not be wandering these streets alone. Where is your MaMa?" he asked softly.

Like the small, fast storms that follow the Mississippi River, Camille fought to keep her anger. She threw her chin up as her hands found their way to her hips. "I am not a child."

Before he could stop himself, his heated gaze dropped to the gentle curve of her bosom, covered as it was with cloth. He swallowed as desire gripped him.

"No, my storm-cloud, no you are not," he replied. "However, there are others who would do you harm, especially because you are not a child."

Nervously, Camille looked about, seeing danger for the first time. Every passerby held some sort of threat, and she clutched worriedly at her cross necklace. She then looked back at the gentleman before her and narrowed her eyes.

"Aye, sir, I do believe you. I'd best be on my—"

"Reece, my boy, so good to see you."

A gentleman's voice boomed from behind her, causing her to jump. Camille whirled around and came face to face with Maggie Lafitte's father. His familiar face instantly eased her nerves.

"Why, Camille. I did not recognize you," the elderly man stammered. Maggie was the sixth of seven children, which put him into his late fifties.

"Mr. Lafitte." Camille smiled prettily. "What a sight for my poor eyes."

"Why, my dear, whatever is the matter?" His brows furrowed with instant worry.

Flipping open her fan, Camille began to wave it in her face as she had seen her MaMa do on several occasions. "I fear I have become separated from Aunt Marie."

"I see. Well, as a gentleman, it is my duty to see you safely to your door, mademoiselle."

At that point, Reece interceded. He cleared his throat, and two pairs of eyes turned to him. "Might I be allowed to help you, sir, escort this lovely lady to safety?"

Mr. Lafitte smiled, instantly recognizing the young man's interest in the girl. He secretly thought they would make an excellent match. "By all means, son, that would be most satisfactory."

* * * *

Unfortunately, Aunt Marie was notoriously bad with directions, and though she had lived in New Orleans her entire life, she always managed to get lost. Thus, she took a left on Iberville Street instead of right and ended up on the riverfront. A bit put out, she bit her lip in worry and hailed a carriage. She would comb the Quarter for her niece, but not on foot.

* * * *

"Perhaps Mrs. Leonhardt has returned home," Mr. Lafitte suggested.

Camille bit her lip in consternation as she peered into the jewelry store. There was absolutely no sign of Aunt Marie. She worked the cross between her fingers and turned to the two men behind her.

"Perhaps," she smiled briefly, worry descending upon her. She had been rash in leaving her Aunt's side. *The poor woman must be having fits by now.*

Mr. Lafitte offered his arm. "To your home then?"

Camille licked her lips. "I do believe I am parched, sir."

The old man nodded. "Yes, I believe a cup of tea would taste delightful. Reece?"

"Yes, sir, I agree."

"Good. There is a place not far from here."

* * * *

An awkward silence fell upon Reece and Camille as they sat at a small table outside of the Shop of Two Sisters. Mr. Lafitte had managed to acquire an on-the-spot invitation from Ms. Camors to partake of tea and cakes in the shop's private courtyard. Then he had left for a spell to conduct a bit of business at the Louisiana State Bank several blocks away.

Before leaving, though, he had arranged for Ms. Bertha Camors, one of the shop's sisters, to chaperone Reece and Camille. Having known Ms. Camors for quite some time, he was more than confident in leaving the two in her hands.

Camille concentrated on a street sign as she fought the urge to stare at Reece's handsome face. She desperately wanted to gaze at him, but she did not want to be thought a silly girl.

Reece watched her discomfort with mild amusement. "Ms. du Carte," he said. "I would ask you a favor."

Her eyes flew to his face, and she caught her breath. She struggled to control her emotions. "Sir?"

He pulled a jewelry box from within his coat and toyed with it. "I," he hesitated. "Would you mind holding onto this for me? I fear bringing it on my ship with me."

He opened the box and placed it in front of her. Dark ruby earrings cast in filigree gold sparkled in the sunlight. The very ones she had so coveted not hours before. Camille's heart jumped in her throat, and her eyes met his.

"They were my mother's. It seems a servant had stolen them, and I recently found them in Waldhorn's shop."

"They're beautiful," she whispered.

"They're an heirloom, and I wish to surprise my mother. However, I am going to sea for several months, and as she lives in Baton Rouge, I will not soon see her."

Camille swallowed, as mischievous thoughts fluttered through her head. If she kept them for him, what harm would it cause if she wore them?

"I'd be forever in your debt, ma chéri," Reece whispered. He waited her reply anxiously. He had his ulterior motives as well. He breathed a sigh of relief as she nodded her consent. He smiled victoriously. He was sure to see her upon his return.

Chapter 2

Nervously, Camille placed the jewelry box on the counter of Waldhorn's. It had been one week since she had met Reece, and she was beside herself. Somehow, during Maggie's party, she had managed to break one of the earrings.

"I need to know if you can fix these."

The clerk smiled at her. "I am sure we can."

Upon opening the box, the clerk's face froze. He glanced briefly at Camille. "Will you excuse me for but a moment?"

A few minutes later, Mr. Waldhorn emerged with the clerk in tow. Oddly, they placed themselves between Camille and the door. The owner's face was red with anger.

"'Tis true, then," he murmured. "They do return to the scene."

Unsure of what he was implying, Camille nervously worked at the cross around her neck. She did not know what she would do if they could not fix the broken earring. Reece would be extremely upset with her.

"Young lady, did you really believe you would get away with it?" Mr. Waldhorn asked.

Camille's brows furrowed. "Away with what, sir?"

He blew air out of his nose in exasperation and placed his hands on his hips. "I am sorry to say, but your plan to slip these earrings back into the store has failed."

"Whatever are you talking about?" Camille asked incredulously. Then it began to sink in.

Mr. Waldhorn grabbed her arm. "Henry, go get a policeman. I believe we have caught our jewelry thief."

* * * *

Camille's face was puffy and red from crying. Her thoughts were a chaotic mess. She had no idea life would turn so quickly on her. If she had that Reece Duponte in front of her, she would claw his eyes out.

All of this was his fault. He had given her stolen jewelry, and since she had them in her possession, Mr. Waldhorn had pressed charges against her. She bit her lower lip to keep the tears at bay.

The door to the sergeant's office opened, and her father walked in. Camille jumped to her feet, but as she was handcuffed to the chair, she was unable to go to him.

Mr. du Carte turned to the sergeant. "Are those really necessary? For God's sake, she's a bare slip of a girl."

The sergeant hurried to do the lawyer's bidding. Seconds later, Camille was crying in her father's arms. Wisely, he let the tears spill a bit before he spoke.

"The jewelry store has no record of selling the earrings to anyone."

Camille sniffed and stepped back from him. She rubbed her wrists where the handcuffs had chafed her skin. "But, PaPa, I swear to you. I did not steal them."

His eyes narrowed. "Aunt Marie told me how much you had wanted them and that when she told you no, you ran off and were unaccountable for hours."

"But, PaPa, I was with Maggie's father, Mr. Lafitte. I swear to you. I did not take them," Camille moaned.

Clay du Carte stared at her, seeing only his daughter instead of the criminal they insisted she was. He knew she was not a thief, but the stolen property had been in her possession. There was no denying that.

"What did this Reece fellow look like, Miss?" the sergeant asked softly.

Camille dabbed at her eyes with her handkerchief. "Well, his name was Reece Duponte, and he was at least a foot taller than I. He had dark hair, and his eyes," she paused, remembering their beauty. She shook her head. He was the reason she was in this mess. She would do well to remember that instead of his handsome eyes.

"His eyes were a violet-blue."

The sergeant looked confused. "Violent blue?"

"Violet," she repeated, but because her nose was so stopped up from crying, it sounded like violent. She had to spell it out for him.

"And how old would you say he was?"

"Twenty."

He jotted the information in his notes. "Do you know where he lives?"

"Someplace in Baton Rouge, but he was going to sea for a month or two," Camille said.

"I don't suppose you know the name of the ship?"

Camille shook her head. She sighed as a weariness fell upon her. At her request, the sergeant brought some water.

Her father sank into the chair beside her and took her hand. "Mr. Waldhorn has refused to drop the charges. I offered to pay for the earrings, but it did not make a difference." He hesitated before continuing. "He also swears that you stole several other pieces that have been missing for several weeks."

Camille sat up straighter. "What? That's preposterous."

He held up his hand for her to hear him out. "Be that as it may, he only has proof of the earrings. I spoke with Judge Calhoun, and you will only be charged with one account of larceny."

Camille's mouth dropped as a cold ball of fear fell into her stomach. "I am to be charged?"

Clay nodded solemnly. "I am afraid that it is so. However, the good news is that this case will not go to trial."

Her face brightened. "Then I may come home?"

"For a time."

Camille's brows drew together. "I don't understand."

Clay grabbed her other hand. "The agreement between the Judge, Mr. Waldhorn and myself is that you serve six months at the Beauregard Plantation in order to avoid a trial."

Camille's jaw dropped further. "I am to serve six months in jail? Can't you just pay the little man the money for the damn earrings and be done with it?"

Clay looked at her reproachfully for her choice of words before shaking his head. "As I said earlier, that is not possible."

He sat back in the chair and sighed. He pulled out a cigar, lit it and inhaled deeply. Then he slowly released the smoke from his lungs. Camille resisted the familiar urge to pull the nasty cigar out of his hands.

"It seems that Mr. Waldhorn has recently been plagued with the disappearance of costume jewelry. At first, he decided not to worry about it as the loss was minimal. Then it became more frequent, and he became more concerned. He and his personnel made an extra effort to keep a watch out for the thief. Strangely enough, the items that were missing then began to turn up days later in the oddest places. It was also noted that there was of late an increase in the patronage of younger ladies, mostly in groups."

Camille's brows furrowed as she recalled a curious conversation between two of her friends at Maggie's birthday party. She had approached Emily and Belle from behind. Their frantic whispering had made her curious. Unfortunately, the only words she had caught were initiate and jewelry. The two had then ceased their discussion when they saw her.

She shook her head free of the memory, tossing it aside like a used handkerchief. She decided not to mention it to her father as it was too vague to be pursued.

Her father absentmindedly blew cigar smoke in her direction, and she waved it away in irritation. Too lost in his own thoughts to notice what he had done, Clay continued talking.

"The Beauregard Plantation is north of Baton Rouge, near St. Francisville. You will be constantly chaperoned by Mrs. Beauregard for the time that you are there."

"What will I do there?" she asked in a small voice.

"Well, with the slaves freed, Mr. Beauregard has arranged for the leasing of prisoners to work on the plantation. They are men who work in the fields. You will in no way be exposed to them. Your duties as the only woman convict—"

"Convict?" Camille gasped, her hand flying to her mouth, mortified. *Oh, dear God.*

Ignoring her outburst, Clay continued. "Your duties will confine you to the house. You will assist Mrs. Beauregard in whatever household task she may require of you."

Silence hung heavily as each struggled to grasp the impossibility of the situation. Camille bit her lower lip as tears sprang to her eyes. "I am ruined. No respectable man shall ever ask for my hand," she whispered.

Clay placed his arm around her and pulled her into a fatherly embrace. The road ahead of them would prove difficult indeed. He kissed the top of her head in reassurance.

Chapter 3

Camille drew the pillow closer, squirming around to find a comfortable position. Then she closed her eyes and took a deep breath, willing her body to relax. For a brief second, there was nothing. No sound. No thoughts. She was lost within the darkness of her bedroom. She hesitated on the brink of sleep, ready to fall headlong into oblivion. Then, one image pulled her back from the edge: Reece's face.

Cold dread rushed through her body. She wiggled around once more, stretching out her legs. Camille couldn't shake the feeling of fear that coursed through her. She pointed her toes as her body tensed in reaction to the fearful adrenaline running rampant. She forced herself to relax, but the horrible events of the day replayed in her head. No matter how much she tossed, they plagued her unmercifully until she jumped out of the bed in frustration.

She pulled her peignoir off a nearby settee and threw it around herself. Then she quietly opened the French doors and stepped out onto her small, private balcony overlooking First Street. Her father had asked her several times not to sit on the balcony in her nightclothes, but she was finding out that certain childhood habits died hard. In order not to arouse his anger further, she quickly sat down, using the railing to hide her presence. Sighing, she looked up at the peaceful night sky, seeking its soothing arms.

Damn that Reece, she thought for the thousandth time. *If I ever see him again, I swear I will scratch those handsome eyes out.*

Tears sprang to her eyes, but she held them in check. She was tired of crying. She was sure that her face would stay red and puffy the rest of her life if she did not stop. Camille angrily swiped away the single drop that had leaked out.

Sighing, she tried to concentrate on something else, which led to the remembrance of her friends' conversation. The words *jewelry* and *initiate* rang warning bells in her head.

Could they possibly be involved in what Mr. Waldhorn had described to Father? If so, for what purpose? Is there some sort of secret society I am not party to? Thankfully not party to.

Camille closed her eyes and leaned her head back. At this moment, she wanted nothing but the sleep that eluded her. Her body, however, was too tense to let her relax. Thoughts of what was to come at the plantation nagged at her brain. *What will they require me to do?*

She supposed that she would be required to do menial housework. *Well, if they expect me to balk at the idea, they have another thing coming.* She decided then that no matter what Mrs. Beauregard asked of her, she would do it to the best of her ability. That would show them what kind of person she truly was, and despite what Mr. Waldhorn thought, Camille knew that she was not a thief. The truth would eventually seep through. She felt confident of it. In the meantime, she would just have to take it one day at a time.

At long last, weariness climbed over her and claimed the adrenaline rush she had been suffering. Her eyes drooped, and she fell asleep curled up in a ball on the balcony.

* * * *

With the coming of dawn came also the noise of a city wakening. Camille's eyes flew open with a start, instantly realizing she was still on the balcony. On hands and knees, she backed up into her bedroom and right into a set of legs. Startled, she looked up into reproachful eyes.

"MaMa," she whispered.

"Camille, you know that your PaPa does not want you out there in your nightclothes. How often must we have this discussion?" the brunette said with a sigh.

Chagrined, Camille scrambled to her feet. She sidestepped around her MaMa and went to wash her face in the nearby basin, hoping that activity would help change the topic of discussion. However, when she faced the room again, Camille knew she was in for a long talk. Her MaMa was sitting upon the settee.

The quiet room was charged with nervous energy. Her MaMa studied her own hands for a long time before finally finding the words. "Your situation has placed a great deal of strain upon this family, Camille."

Tears immediately sprang to her eyes, and Camille bit her lip to keep them from spilling. She threw her chin out and waited for the undeserved lecture she was about to receive.

"We are as yet undecided on a course of action upon your return. There are several options." At this, her MaMa paused. "Your reputation has been ruined."

For the first time, a bitterness of her mother's elite society rose up in Camille, and she looked upon its inmates with a different light. It was no longer just mere gossip to titter about. Now, it was high gossip about her that would only become more scandalous upon her return from her 'term of service'. The full realization that life-changing consequences would result from this unfortunate event crashed down upon her young shoulders. She sank to the floor as her legs became weak.

"I thought it best that you know that one of the possibilities is boarding school," her MaMa continued. Camille waved her hand as if in dismissal of the idea. "But that is just one of many."

"What of Mr. Lafitte? Did PaPa have a chance to speak with him?"

Her mother's eyes grew colder. "Yes, he did, and Mr. Lafitte confirmed that Reece Duponte was a business associate of his. However, he has no knowledge of Reece's family, only that they live somewhere around Baton Rouge. He also did not remember Reece giving you the earrings."

Camille frowned. "Of course not. He was at the bank. We were waiting for him in the courtyard of The Shop of Two Sisters."

Her mother sat forward with sudden anticipation. "Then Ms. Camors was in attendance?"

Camille nodded. "She was, but she had gone inside to help with customers for a brief period. It was then that Reece gave me the earrings."

Dejected, she sat back in the chair and stared at the ceiling. "Then she will be no help at all."

After a moment of silence, her MaMa stood. "The seamstress will be here shortly to measure you for your wardrobe."

Camille quickly rose to her feet and forced herself to approach her socialite MaMa. Gray eyes looked pleadingly into blue ones, and as the wall between them crashed, they embraced in a hug that seemed to last forever.

"I love you, Camille, and I will do all that is in my power to help you," her MaMa whispered painfully.

"I love you, too, MaMa."

* * * *

Camille frowned at the officer blocking her path to the outside world. He looked very formidable in his refusal to let her out, and no amount of flirtation pierced the armor he wore. Frustrated, she slammed the door in his face, gaining some satisfaction from her momentary act of defiance. Then she threw her hat at the door and huffed back upstairs to her bedroom. The second door slamming brought her even more satisfaction, and the child in her rose to the surface. She opened her bedroom door and slammed it several times in an effort to relieve her pent-up aggravation.

As her rage grew out of control, Camille grabbed a nearby clock, pulled open the doors and dropped it over the side of her balcony. The startled guard hurried out into the street and looked up. When he realized it was her, his face darkened, and he disappeared into the house.

The blood drained from her face as she realized what a rash act that had been, and she turned to lock her bedroom door before the officer could come in. The sight of her father stopped her in her tracks.

"PaPa." The word stuck in her throat.

"Camille, may I ask what the devil has gotten in to you?"

She forced her eyes to the floor in an effort to remain calm as the so-called-devil rose once more to the surface. "All I wanted was to take a walk."

The officer appeared in the doorway. "Is there anything I can do?"

She glared at him. "He would not let me leave."

Clay looked from her to the police officer and then back at his daughter. "He is doing his job, Camille. You are under house arrest, which means you cannot leave on your own."

She crossed her arms, and her mouth became a grim line. "Fine."

The room became permeated with her anger. The two men decided a hasty retreat was in order, and the door closed quietly behind them. Camille paced the room and ended up once more on the balcony.

She had not understood until then how much her life had become the property of others. She no longer had the privilege that freedom entailed. The walls of her prison had begun the moment she had left the police station. She just had not felt them touch her shoulders until now.

Gloomily, Camille leaned on the rail of her balcony, watching the people as they meandered by. She had planned to make a call on Maggie Lafitte to see if her younger friend knew anything about the conversation Camille had overheard. *It's probably just as well. Maggie probably would have shunned me anyway.*

A weight settled in her heart, and her mind went to the source of her problem: violet-blue eyes. For the thousandth time, she went over the conversations she had with Reece but nothing came to mind. She could not remember if he had even mentioned the name of the ship he was supposedly working on.

She grunted in agitation and pushed away from the rail. The piano downstairs called to her as it always did when she was in the midst of a problem. Camille knew everything would melt away while she played, and she hurried to seek temporary relief from her tumultuous thoughts.

* * * *

A soft tapping caused Camille to pause in her reading. Sighing, she opened the bedroom door to find her MaMa.

"You have a guest awaiting you in the parlor." She paused. "Maggie Lafitte."

Camille's eyes lit up, and she hurried past her MaMa. *Thank God,* she thought as she ran down the stairs. *Finally, someone to talk to.*

Hesitating before the closed parlor doors, Camille took a deep breath and then entered. Her best friend was already indulging in tea and cakes, and Camille poured herself some tea, forcing her hands not to shake. When she finally looked at Maggie's pale face, she noticed the girl was close to tears.

"Don't," Camille warned. "For if you get me going, I fear I

shall never stop."

"Oh, Camie, I cannot believe this has happened," Maggie moaned softly. An uncomfortable silence quickly fell upon the two. "How long will you be gone?"

"Six months."

"Oh, my," Maggie whispered. She grabbed Camille's hand and tried to smile. "I shall see to it that not a soul will tempt Brent's heart."

A little guiltily, Camille realized with a start that she had not once thought of Brent Lafourche. She also took note that he had not called since her unfortunate situation. Camille smiled weakly and simply nodded at Maggie. She had a feeling she had seen the last of that one.

"Camie, there's something I must confess."

As Camille threw her a curious look, the doors to the parlor swung open, conveniently stopping their intimate discussion. Emily St. Amande filled the doorway with the imposing stature of a dominant queen. Her eyes locked on Maggie's face with a warning while her words were directed at Camille.

"Dear Camie, I came as soon as I heard."

Camille stood as the red-head rushed to her side. She graciously accepted the offered hug, but she doubted the sincerity of her newest guest. After offering tea and cakes, the trio was drawn into a conversation dominated by Emily. The rest of the afternoon became wasted on questions and gossip. Maggie's confession was put on the back burner indefinitely as Emily insisted she accompany her home.

Disappointed, Camille watched them from the window as they hurried out of sight. She had a nagging suspicion that Maggie was about to divulge information in regards to the overheard conversation. Unfortunately, as she was leaving in the morning, it would be six months before she saw her best friend again.

Chapter 4

July 1, 1889

Camille's stomach was twisted up in knots. She stood beside her father as her one and only trunk was loaded onto the carriage. Her shoulders drooped, and the corners of her mouth were turned down.

She was being punished for a crime she hadn't committed. She felt like a trapped animal. The thought of running away had crossed her mind several times over the past week, but with two policemen dogging her every step, there had been no opportunity. Not that she would have run away. Deep down, she was the type to stare her problems in the face, not run and hide.

Swallowing over the lump in her throat, Camille turned to look at her home one more time. It was very early in the morning, about four thirty, and the sun had hours yet to rise. Clay had thought it prudent to have this exchange happen as early as possible in order to prevent neighborly curiosity. As such, all Camille could see of the house was darkened shadows.

She sighed, thinking of her mother. They had exchanged farewells inside, both with stiff upper lips. *That stubborn du Carte pride*, she thought wistfully.

The sergeant looked at the sky before indicating it was time to go. Camille kissed her father on his cheek before throwing her arms around him in a childlike manner.

"I am so sorry, PaPa," she whispered.

Clay rubbed her back gently. "Shhh. I will have the docks watched, ma chéri. If that man returns, I will do everything in my power to set things right." He held her at arms length. "I believe you, Camille."

Clay helped his youngest daughter into the coach and then turned to the matronly woman beside him. Her features were set in a hardened fashion, and he knew it was her winning personality that had kept her a spinster for fifty some odd years. However, he knew she would provide adequate chaperoning for the trip to Beauregard Plantation.

"Ms. Ridgemont, thank you again for accompanying Camille."

"You are quite welcome, Monsieur du Carte," she replied, allowing him to assist her into the coach. Any other man, she would have slapped his hand away, but she had a huge amount of respect for Clay du Carte and so let him aid her portly ascent. After Sergeant O'Connell and his two officers got into the coach, they began their journey.

* * * *

Nervously, Camille smoothed out the wrinkles of her gray dress. Her trunk was filled with similar gray dresses, which had been made specifically for her 'term of service.'

Gray, gray, gray, she thought as depression got the best of her.

"Won't be long now, Miss," Sergeant O'Connell said. "Beauregard's just up the road a bit."

He smiled encouragingly, not liking the paleness of her skin. He felt sorry for the lass, but there was nothing he could do. 'Twas a pity Mr. Waldhorn had made such a fuss over a pair of earrings.

A little embarrassed, he pulled out the handcuffs. He

cleared his throat. "Um, I'll be needing to put these on ya now, Miss. 'Tis customary for the prisoner to be wearing them."

Camille's eyes grew wide at the word *prisoner*. Reluctantly, she forced her hands out in front of her. She turned her head and closed her eyes as the heavy things were locked about her dainty wrists.

Damn. Those bruises had just begun to fade.

The carriage rolled to a stop, and the sergeant helped Ms. Ridgemont and Camille out. Her mouth fell as she realized with a start that she had been delivered to the servants' door. Her pride pummeled even further, and her chin sunk a little closer to her chest. *The ultimate disgrace.* Camille was accustomed to being received at the front door. She had never stopped to consider just how low this Reece fellow had caused her to sink. Her eyes narrowed as her heart overflowed with hate.

A young, dark-skinned maid answered the door and immediately stepped aside to let them enter. The little group moved into the food preparation room. Since the actual kitchen was completely separate from the house, the servants used this area to ready the meal for serving. It also served as a gathering area for the servants when they weren't busy.

As the maid went to fetch Mrs. Beauregard, Camille looked around in curiosity. This was to be her home for six months. She envisioned hours slaving away at some menial house chore or another. She threw up her chin, determined not to let the situation get the best of her.

"So this is our little jewelry thief?"

All eyes focused on the matronly figure in the doorway. Mrs. Beauregard was a foot taller than Camille. Her black hair had touches of gray scattered throughout, and her blue eyes calmly assessed the young girl before her.

Sergeant O'Connell stepped forward. "Mrs. Beauregard, may I present Miss Camille du Carte."

"Hello, Miss du Carte."

Mindful of her manners, Camille responded with politeness. "It is a pleasure to meet you, ma'am."

In her mind, though, she would rather not have met anyone this way. She dared a glance at the older woman's face, but what she saw was not dislike as she had expected. Instead, there was an air of curiosity that Camille suspected was out of character for Mrs. Beauregard.

"Well, sergeant, I shall see that you and your entourage are properly fed before you leave. Fran," the woman turned to the young servant, "run out to the kitchen and have Mrs. Smith whip something together for them. Sergeant, I believe those are no longer necessary."

Mrs. Beauregard pointed at Camille's cuffed hands, and the man hurried to release his prisoner. Gratefully, Camille rubbed her wrists as she followed her caretaker to a locked door on the other side of the room.

"This is your room for your stay with us," Mrs. Beauregard said while unlocking the door. "There have been other women here before you, and as my husband has a contract with the penitentiary, we routinely buy the services of those unfortunates such as yourself."

Camille stepped into a room that was one-third the size of her room at home. There was a window with bars to her left. Before her was a small bed and to her right was a siphon closet. At least she would not have to use the old fashioned chamber pot.

"Each night, you will be locked in here, as you are still a prisoner of the state and, therefore, cannot be allowed to roam free."

A bit detached, Camille followed Mrs. Beauregard through the dining room. The huge dark table was sturdy but beautiful. There was a mirror on one wall, and the sight of herself startled her. She looked awfully thin, which wasn't surprising since her appetite had melted to almost nothing. There were dark circles under her eyes, and her skin looked taut. If she were at home, her mother would have set her up in a room full of steam. She sighed heavily and trudged along to the next room.

As the parlor faced the morning sun, the room was darkened in shadows. Fortunately, she noticed there was no bric-a-brac for her to dust around. Two sets of French doors led to the immense porch.

"The family gathers on the porch on warm summer evenings," Mrs. Beauregard stated. "You will be required to help Fran serve the lemonade."

The two crossed the hall, and Camille felt a jolt of excitement surge through her. A beautiful black grand piano sat in front of the French doors. She looked furtively at Mrs. Beauregard, wondering if she would ever be allowed to play. She secretly hoped so.

"This is the music room. Little Annie practices much throughout the day, so you might have to dust around her." The woman smiled at the thought. Although the matron tried to keep a stern look about her, her face brightened warmly for a brief second. Camille dared to hope that she would not be as stern as she had feared.

The matron paused at the stairs. "Your services will not be required upstairs."

Camille could practically see the wheels turning in her head. *The family jewels must be kept somewhere upstairs.* Her heart dipped in remembrance of what had brought her here. Her eyes narrowed at the thought of violet-blue eyes.

The study would be the hardest place to dust due to all the volumes and texts. The desk was customarily locked at all times, not just because a 'thief' was now in their midst.

When they returned to the kitchen, a plate of steaming

food waited for her. Her stomach rumbled at the smell, and at Mrs. Beauregard's indication, she sat at the servant's table. Camille closed her eyes, folded her hands and whispered a small prayer before eating.

The dark-skinned servant waited patiently against the wall, and Mrs. Beauregard sat beside her newest servant. "Fran has been instructed not to leave you unattended. Please do not try to escape. For the time being, I will not insist on the handcuffs, but if you try to escape, we will have to take the necessary precautions a step further."

Camille nervously swallowed the food in her mouth as her appetite vanished. She pushed around the remains on her plate, acutely aware that she had barely eaten half. Her eyes met Mrs. Beauregard's, and before the matron could make any comment on wasted food, Camille forced the rest of it down. She felt like regurgitating but managed to keep it down. She was led once again to her room.

"I'm sorry, but I cannot trust you with a candle. I'm sure you understand why." Mrs. Beauregard looked at the window where a gaslight flamed brightly just beyond reach. "The light will be extinguished approximately thirty minutes after we have settled you in for the night. We are early risers, my dear."

Camille hugged herself as the door closed softly and the keys jangled in the lock. The gaslight lit the room a good bit, and she noticed that her trunk had been set at the foot of her bed. Homesick, the first tear finally slipped past her steel resolve and the rest poured in a silent stream down her face. She sank onto the bed and buried her face into the pillow.

Chapter 5

Third week of July

Each time Camille dusted the piano, the urge to play was overwhelming. However, she managed to curb the impulse and listen to the voice in her head that told her to wait.

It had been three weeks since her arrival, and so far, she had managed to stay out of trouble. She had even struck up a friendship of sorts with Fran and the rest of the servants. Nights were the hardest, and on occasion, the tears were absent. She even had gained some of her appetite back, but she knew that was due to all the housework.

Little Annie proved to be a very sweet and talented young lady. The eight-year-old had a question for everything and sometimes an answer as well. Camille did notice the child was adventurous as she often came in from playing with dirt and mud all over her shoes and dress. Yet no matter how much her mother fussed, Annie would repeat the performance the very next day.

At the moment, she was practicing her scales on the piano. For thirty minutes, she raced her fingers up and down the ivory keys. She was quite talented, but Camille secretly felt she had outgrown her current teacher. The child needed more advanced training if she were to get better than she already was.

Abruptly, Annie stopped and fixed her gaze on Camille, who lingered on the other side of the room.

"Do you play, Miss Camille?" The child's voice echoed loudly in the room, and Camille looked nervously toward the door, waiting for Mrs. Beauregard to appear. She knew the lady was in the parlor knitting and would hear every word.

"Yes, Miss Annie, I have played since I was four."

The little girl's eyes widened in awe. "You must be very good."

A blush crept into Camille's cheeks. "Well, I have been told so."

"Will you play for me?"

Camille's breath caught in her throat. "I, uh, I…"

Before she had a chance to finish her sentence, a presence filled the doorway. She looked into the older woman's face, expecting harshness but instead found curiosity.

"I would be delighted as well to hear you play, Miss du Carte," the lady stated quietly.

Camille was more than happy to oblige. She quickly set her cleaning rag on the floor as Annie jumped from the bench. Nervously, she sat at the piano and began to play the first piece that came to mind.

"Before I left home, I was perfecting my Beethoven. This was dedicated to the Baroness Josefine von Braun, Allegro Number Ten in G major."

Peace eased the lines of worry on Camille's face as she played, and she became lost in the music. When the piece was finished, she came back to reality with a sudden clarity. The clapping drew her attention to Annie and Mrs. Beauregard.

Her cheeks rosy, Camille dipped her head slightly. "Thank you."

"My dear, you are quite accomplished," Mrs. Beauregard

stated. "Do you know any others?"

A dazzling smile that hadn't been seen in months spread across Camille's face as she nodded. Chores were pushed aside as the rest of the afternoon was dedicated to Beethoven, Chopin and New Orleans' most recent pianist, Henry Whermann, Jr.

* * * *

He plagued Camille's dreams each and every night. The scoundrel stood behind Mr. Waldhorn and laughed silently as the jeweler placed the handcuffs on her wrists. Then, Emily would appear beside him and link her arm through his in a conspiratorial manner. Once, she even dreamt of Reece kissing Emily and was astonished at the jealousy rising in her.

One night, she dreamt that she was locked in his embrace while he kissed her thoroughly and completely. When he released her, she realized there was something in her mouth. She then spit out the damned ruby earrings.

Tonight was no respite to his dream pursuit of her. He had followed her once more into sleep.

"I hate you," she screamed into violet-blue eyes. "It's your fault that I am in such a mess. My reputation is ruined. No man will marry me now."

She flew at him in a rage and pummeled his chest with her small fists. Tears poured down her face as unladylike words escaped her lips.

He grabbed her delicate wrists. The warmth of his strong, weather-beaten hands shocked her, as she recognized that she was dreaming. Her eyes met his as her words died on the tip of her tongue. His heated gaze suddenly sent unwanted desire plummeting through her, and she felt herself relax in his grip.

Slowly, he lowered his head, and for some odd reason, she made no protest when his soft lips found hers. She melted against him as her body won the fight with her mind.

Reece let go of her wrists and wrapped one arm around her waist, pulling her close. His other hand found her breast, and his thumb grazed her nipple. Her body jerked as an inner flame blazed down her stomach to her womanhood. As it awakened for the first time, she wriggled against him, wanting something she could not yet give a name to.

"My little storm," he whispered against her hair. "So full of unreleased lightning."

Then, he abruptly let go of her and stepped back into the rising fog. Camille cried out in protest. She took a step forward and was immediately thrown back on the ground. She sat up, only to find herself awake in her bed.

Now where on earth had that come from? Never in my life... The wanton feelings still trembled through her. Blushing, she pushed the remnants of the dream from her head and tried to sleep.

* * * *

"My brother plays as well as you." Annie smiled as she sipped her lemonade.

Time at the piano had drawn Camille and the little girl close. Consequently, time had passed more quickly for Camille as Mrs. Beauregard allowed her to tutor Annie after the chores were done. She was even allowed on the porch for a glass of lemonade after lessons.

"Really? And what is your brother's name?" Camille asked as a cool breeze caressed her skin. Fall was upon them.

"Aristodemus," Annie replied, carefully pronouncing each word.

Camille raised a curious eyebrow, and Annie giggled. "His father loved Greek mythology."

Camille nodded knowingly. "I see." Then it dawned on her. "His father and your father are not one and the same?"

"No, ma'am. His father died."

"Oh, I'm sorry to hear that."

Taking a sip of lemonade, Camille thought of her own father so far away. She had a stack of letters in her room from both her parents and a few from her sister. Maggie had written her several times as well. Homesick, she focused her attention on the young girl beside her.

The child was prattling on about her brother, and Camille realized she had tuned her out and lost part of the conversation. "I'm sorry, Annie. What were you saying?"

"My brother is very handsome," she smiled, cunning in her young eyes. Camille immediately knew what she was up to but pretended not to notice.

"I am sure he is."

"He'll be home any day now, and he promised to bring me something." Annie jumped off the swing and searched the carriage lane for any sign of him. Camille smiled, seeing the adoration Annie had for her older brother.

Five minutes later, Camille rose to her feet. It was time to help with dinner preparations. She followed her ever-present companion, Fran, into the house.

Chapter 6

Beginning of September

The clanking of keys brought Camille out of her dream. Sleepily, she sat up in her bed as the door swung open, and Annie practically fell into the room. The child's face was flushed with excitement as she bounced eagerly on the bed. Camille raised a tired eyebrow at the youngster's choice of clothing.

"I hope you do not expect me to wear such outlandish clothing as well."

Annie put on an air of practicality. "But Camille, fishing is a messy job. Do you really want your dresses mussed with mud and worm guts?"

Camille wrinkled her nose. "I shall be content to let you bait my hook."

Annie laughed and shook her head. "No way. Why, that is the fun of fishing. Besides, a real fisher-woman baits her own hook."

Camille yawned and raised her arms in a healthy stretch. "Alright, Miss Annie, if you will excuse me so that I may get dressed."

Camille smiled and shook her head as Annie scampered out of the room. She knew the child was anxious to get to the pond. As she dressed, she wondered vaguely how much the child had pestered her father to let her go with them. Although Camille had not been fishing since she was a young girl, she found she looked forward to this little venture. A break from the normality would be refreshing.

When she stepped from her room, a warm cup of coffee was thrust into her hands. Then Annie ushered her out of the house and onto the front porch where Mr. Beauregard awaited them. He too held a cup of hot coffee and smiled weakly at Camille.

"Children," he murmured.

Camille returned his grin and raised her cup. "I second that."

"Shall we then?"

Camille nodded and followed Annie as she danced down the stairs of the porch. The dark sky had begun to lighten with the coming dawn. A chilly wind whipped around them, and Camille clung to the warmth of the mug. Mr. Beauregard carried three fishing poles, and Annie carried a small shovel for digging up fresh worms. The child had made a small worm bed from a wooden crate. Camille recalled how Annie had been extremely proud of her accomplishment.

She thought of the fishing trips with her own father. Lake Pontchartrain had seen her often as a child, but upon reaching her debutante years, mother had insisted that the trips end. Camille missed those trips.

Golden innocent years, she thought yearningly.

As they walked through the woods, the damp, cold air seemed to sink through the skin and into the bones. Camille set the empty cup on the path, making a mental note to pick it up on their return trip. She then shoved her hands into the pockets of her heavy coat. She was glad it wasn't made of the highest quality, as she knew the trip would prove messy. Her mother had thoughtfully sent her with one nice and one practical coat.

Upon reaching the pond, Mr. Beauregard helped her ready the fishing pole. He even hooked the worm for her and threw the line in the water. Then he moved farther down to set up his own line.

By that time, daylight had arrived, but the fish had yet to bite. Camille kept as still as possible, remembering the need for silence. She waited for the telltale bump that indicated a fish was hunting her worm. The minutes dragged slowly by, and Camille risked glancing up to check out the sky.

The second she raised her eyes, the pole in her hand jumped, and she jerked the tip up, reeling as fast as she could. A hand-sized sun-perch soon flopped on the ground before her.

Smiling, Camille looked for her companions, only to find both of them almost on the other side of the pond. It was up to her to remove the slimy fish. While she wasn't squeamish, she wrinkled her nose from the smell. Then, taking a deep breath, she knelt down, firmly grabbed the fish between her fingers and pried the hook out of its mouth. Mr. Beauregard had left her with a stringer line to keep the fish she caught, and after she threaded it through the fish's mouth and out of its gill, she set it in the water close to the edge.

The rest of the morning flew by, and on the way back, all three had a string full of fish to carry. Stomachs rumbled as each wondered how the cook would prepare them. A feeling of camaraderie settled over Camille, and she began to feel more like a part of the family than a convict. Her reserve slipped, and she was amazed to realize how relaxed she felt. The fishing trip had served to help ease her nerves. She looked at the back of Annie's head and tears sprang to her eyes. The little girl had unwittingly helped her, and her heart warmed at the thought.

* * * *

"Camille, would you please call for Annie?" Mrs. Beauregard asked. "It will be dark soon, and she needs to come in and get ready for dinner."

Camille nodded. "Yes, ma'am."

Over the past months, she had managed to gain the trust of the Beauregard's. Thus, Fran was no longer required to dog her every step. She was proud of this accomplishment and determined to keep her behavior up.

She stepped onto the front porch and began calling for the little girl. Receiving no response, she headed toward the woods. It was quite likely that Annie was at the fishing pond, hunting for frogs or some such thing.

The minute Camille stepped onto the wooded path, the world seemed to change. Quietness enveloped her, and she wrapped her arms about herself as a shiver ran through her. Even the animals were silent. Her imagination soon got the best of her, and she stopped when she thought she heard someone behind her.

After double-checking, Camille chided herself for being foolish and continued on her way. The pond was not far away, and with any luck, Annie would be on this side of it.

As she stepped into the clearing, the hair on the back of her neck rose. Camille turned her head toward a rustling sound to her left and stifled a gasp at the sight of a man holding Annie by her arms. His back was to her. Frantically, she looked about her for a weapon. Tree limb in hand, she ran over and cracked it over his back. Unfortunately, the rotten limb broke in half, but she now had his undivided attention. With a growl, he turned toward her.

"Run, Annie!" Camille screamed, backing away from the man. She recognized him as one of the prisoners used in the fields.

He leered at her. "I knew you'd come after her."

When she stepped in ice cold water, she glanced back and confirmed her suspicion. The pond was right behind her. The big bloke before her continued his approach. She narrowed her eyes and pointed at him.

"Stay away from me," she growled.

"Or what? You'll give me a thrashing I'll never forget?" He smiled wide, revealing rotting teeth. "That would please me much."

Camille blanched, only guessing at his vulgarity. Deciding the water was safer, she dove in and attempted to swim. Unfortunately, the cotton dress clung to her legs, and she found herself sinking. She thrashed about as fear of drowning overcame her.

A pair of rough hands grabbed her arms and pulled her out of the treacherous water. He threw her on the ground and stood dominantly over her. "Stupid woman," he muttered.

Her entire body shook from fear as well as from cold. Her wet bodice clung tightly to her heaving bosom, and she felt completely vulnerable as the letch looked her over from head to toe.

"Cold are ye, miss?"

He dropped to the ground atop her, his knees straddling her. She drew her arms over her chest, and he laughed. The weight of his body did indeed give her warmth, but at the moment, she would have gladly frozen to death. She opened her mouth to scream, but a calloused hand clamped over her lips. Camille tried to buck and fight, but the water had taken all of her strength. She whimpered as he began pushing her skirts up around her waist.

"All the prisoners have an eye fer ye," he whispered as his foul breath filled her nose. "The prettiest little convict I've ever had the privilege to meet."

Closing her eyes, she willed her body to relax. She realized now that fighting would only excite him. A tear escaped her eye and slid down her cheek. She prayed Annie would send help quickly. Swallowing over a lump, bile rose in her throat as she thanked God she had stumbled upon them before he had done this to little Annie. Better it was she than the eight-year-old. Disgust and contempt rose to the surface. If she lived, she would see this man dead.

A loud gunshot filled the clearing. The prisoner stopped his filthy pawing and looked to the path. Camille followed his gaze. Mr. Beauregard pointed a shotgun at the scoundrel's head.

"Close your eyes, Camille!" he yelled as another loud shot rang through the air.

The next thing she knew, the rapist fell to her left. She scrambled to her feet and stared in horror at the dead man. Mr. Beauregard soon stood by her side and put a fatherly arm around her.

"Are you alright?"

Numbly, she nodded, leaning against him for support. He sighed, "I'm sorry. He escaped this morning, and I thought the scoundrel was long gone."

* * * *

A light tapping on her bedroom door pulled Camille back to reality with a start. She had been allowed to rest the entire afternoon, but all she had been able to do was replay the horrible event over and over.

On bare feet, she tiptoed to the door. As it was after nine, all the lights had been turned off, and everyone had supposedly retired for the night. "Who is it?"

"Miss Camille, it's Annie. Can I sleep with you?"

Relief flooded through her, and she quickly moved the chair away from the door. Her fear had motivated her to barricade herself in her room. Though she knew the man was dead, she simply felt the need for some extra protection.

After letting the child in, she replaced the chair, and they got into bed. Camille pulled Annie close, comforted by her presence. Quiet descended upon the room. The child's voice trembled as she spoke. "Daddy told me I must never go anywhere alone anymore. He said I was a very lucky little girl."

"Yes, we both were."

Camille thought of her own father, and her heart ached for his nearness. Perhaps in the morning, she would be allowed to call him on the telephone. What she wouldn't do right now just to smell one of his stinky cigars. A tear spun from homesickness trickled down her face, and she sniffed.

Annie patted her hand comfortingly. "It'll be okay. I feel much better now that I'm with you."

The girl yawned, and Camille followed suit. Weariness climbed over the two, and they fell asleep almost simultaneously.

Chapter 7

Beginning of October

After the episode in the woods, Annie never strayed far from the house by herself. In fact, she became Camille's shadow. The bond between them grew, and for the first time, Camille realized how her own older sister must have felt before she married. There were times when she needed a break from the constant and often-demanding attention of the eight-year-old, but for the most part, it was a wonderful relationship.

At the moment, the two had just returned from the pumpkin patch. Another two weeks would see the entire porch covered with jack-o-lanterns. Then, after Halloween, the uncut ones would be used to make pies for Thanksgiving. Camille's mouth watered at the thought.

Once inside the house, the two separated. Annie ran upstairs to attend to her studies. Her tutor would arrive soon, and the child had forgotten to complete an exercise.

Camille immediately went to the front parlor and commenced her chores. A knock on the front door startled her momentarily. Assuming it was the tutor, Mrs. Robillard, Camille answered it.

Her mouth dropped, and her heart lurched. The face that

plagued her night after night stood before her. She spoke the only word she could think of.

"You!"

Her face filled with fury, but before she had a chance to explode, the unhealthy glaze in Reece's eyes caused her to bite back the words. He leaned against the doorframe, unable to hold himself up. His tanned skin held a tint of yellow, and the sweat on his brow was not from his long walk up the lane.

If he recognized her, she could not tell as he chose that moment to pass out. She instinctively grabbed his shirt as he started to topple back, only to realize too late that he was taking her down with him. Thus, she ended up sprawled on top of him in a most unladylike fashion. She silently thanked God that he was unconscious.

Fran appeared at her elbow and assisted her to her feet. Then, taking one look at Reece, the maid raced to fetch Mrs. Beauregard.

* * * *

As Mrs. Beauregard shut the door behind Dr. Sanderson, Camille waited by the foot of the stairs. Her emotions were torn in two. Her instincts cried out for her to nurse Reece back to health. However, she also wanted to tear every piece of hair off his head. She watched the older lady take a deep breath before facing her. Lifting her chin, she walked past, heading back up stairs.

"Mrs. Beauregard," Camille whispered.

The lady paused and looked down. "Yes?"

"What did the doctor say?"

"My son has a very bad case of Bronze John."

Mrs. Beauregard then continued up as Camille digested the shocking news. Aristodemus was Reece. Reece was Aristodemus. He was Annie's older brother. She cursed and blessed Lady Fate at the same time. Hope then rose within her. Surely, he would help set things straight, but she would have to bide her time and wait until he was well from the yellow fever.

Mrs. Beauregard suddenly appeared in front of her. Grabbing Camille's hand, the lady led her up to the forbidden second floor. Her help was needed, and damn the rules.

* * * *

Reece lay on a mahogany bed beneath layers of mosquito netting. He had tossed his covers aside and was within the hands of the fever. He mumbled unintelligibly in his restless sleep.

Camille sat in a chair as far from him as she could get. The chair swallowed her in its masculinity, and Camille's gaze wandered about the definitely male room. She had never been in a man's bedroom before, and even though Fran was there as well, she felt vulnerable and completely ill at ease.

Fran reached through the net and pressed a cool rag against his forehead. He moaned, then grabbed her hand and pulled her close. His eyes wildly searched her face.

"Where's storm?"

Fran's eyes grew wide, and she tried unsuccessfully to pull away. "There be no storm, sir."

His eyes narrowed. "No storm?"

Fran shook her head, and he dropped back onto the bed. The maid looked quizzically at Camille and then shrugged her shoulders. "He be out o' his mind. That's for sure, Miss."

Camille just stared blankly at her. She had no idea why Mrs. Beauregard asked her to help. She was a city girl and had no idea how to help the sick. There was only one servant who lived with the du Carte's. The rest had their own homes and tended to their own sick. Plantation life was different, as she was quickly coming to learn.

Camille reflected on Reece's prognosis. The doctor had

told Mrs. Beauregard that he would get much worse before he got better. Observing the pitiful state he was in now, she wondered just how much 'worse' was going to be.

The door swung open, and Mrs. Beauregard entered the room. She closed the door softly behind her and leaned back against it. She looked at Fran, then at Camille.

"Well, girls, it's just the three of us now," Mrs. Beauregard sighed. "I sent Mr. Beauregard and Annie to nearby relations. I've ordered the rest of the servants not to set foot inside this house. They are to ring the bell and set our food just inside the door."

The room was quiet as each contemplated the quarantine. Sadly, Camille thought of the plump pumpkins waiting to be harvested. Not even the field hands were allowed to approach the house. There would not be a Halloween party at the plantation this year. Her heart felt a bit heavy as she realized she had not been allowed to tell Annie goodbye.

A cool breeze swept through the room from the open window. Mrs. Beauregard had mosquito netting attached on each window, and doors made of the same material were on every entrance.

"Dr. Sanderson placed a yellow flag on the front porch and at the back door," Mrs. Beauregard stated in a monotone voice. "We are officially quarantined."

Camille watched the play of emotions on the lady's face, and as tears formed in Mrs. Beauregard's eyes, so did they in Camille's, if only out of empathy. Camille rose slowly and closed the space between them. Tentatively, she grabbed Mrs. Beauregard's hand and looked her in the eye.

With trembling lips, she said, "Don't worry, Mrs. Beauregard. We will see him well."

"I hope so, Camille. I cannot lose another to this King of Terror."

* * * *

During the next few days, Reece's condition did indeed worsen. His fever rose and dropped sporadically. He complained of headaches, backaches and nausea. The doctor gave him regular doses of quinine as well as laudanum to relieve pain. It also helped his restlessness, enabling him to sleep deeply instead of dancing in his bed.

Thankfully, Mrs. Beauregard and Fran took care of most of the nursing. Camille was only required to run back and forth for various things such as fresh water, clean rags, broth, et cetera. Thus, she was not called upon to approach Reece's side. Until the day Fran turned up sick.

Mrs. Beauregard thrust the cold rag into Camille's hand before leading Fran to a makeshift cot in a corner of the room. She had decided to keep the sickness in one room for obvious reasons. Then she left to have the doctor summoned again.

With wide eyes, Camille slowly approached Reece's bed. His fever still plagued him, yet he was, to her relief, asleep. Tentatively, she reached through the netting and patted his forehead with the wet rag. Mumbling, he turned on his side, allowing her a better view of his face.

She stared at him, pushing down the frustration and anger that rose in her. His face looked innocent, despite the growth of beard. He raised his hand and pushed the rag off his forehead.

"Storm," Reece whispered, caught in the throes of some nightmare. "Get out of the way. The mast."

Before she had a chance to move, Reece lunged toward her, grabbed her and pulled her across him. She ended up underneath him, trapped in mosquito netting. He looked at her, eyes clear for the first time in days.

"You," he whispered. "Am I still dreaming?"

Without waiting for a response, he pressed his lips against

hers. The presence of the mosquito netting brought him quickly to his senses. He pulled away from her.

"Aye, you are quite real."

His kiss had caught her like a doe in a hunter's path, despite the barrier of netting. When he moved, however, she quickly came to herself. She struggled with the netting, and in her effort, fell flat on her rump beside the bed.

She glanced up at Reece with an angry look, only to become angrier at his look of amusement. In a fury, she finally succeeded in throwing off the netting and got to her feet as gracefully as possible. She smoothed down her skirts, and with her chin in the air, she put a room's distance between them. If her hair had not been so messed up, the effect would have had more impact. Unfortunately, it not only made Reece smile but Fran as well, sick as she was.

"Well," Camille huffed, crossing her arms. "It's about time you woke up."

"Well," Reece responded. "If I had been aware that you were my nurse, perhaps I would have done so sooner."

Giving him a dubious look, she found her eyes lingering too long on his bare chest. Some remnant of a dream stirred in her head, and an unwelcome warmth spread throughout her body. Her cheeks flamed red, and her eyes met his knowing ones.

Gasping, she turned her back on him. The fact that he had thrown his covers here and there in his illness became inconsequential. Now that he was in his right mind, his state of undress was clearly inappropriate.

Unable to resist, Reece mischievously jumped from the bed, walking all over the room in an obviously blatant effort to find a set of clothes. Camille gasped again and pulled open the door, only to come face to face with Mrs. Beauregard and the doctor.

Reece instantly looked like a cat with the pet canary in his mouth. His mother raised an eyebrow at him and stepped aside to let her charge escape. While Reece hurriedly dressed, his mother and the doctor tended to the newest patient. He was about to chase after Camille when weakness rushed over him, and he sank into the nearest chair, flushed.

Dr. Sanderson then appeared at his side, quickly giving him a brief examination. "Well, lad, you've beaten Bronze John, for the time being, anyway. I suggest if you don't want a relapse, that you climb back into that bed and be a good boy."

Reece smiled weakly at the reference to him being a boy. Doc was fifty-something years old, and Reece realized that he'd always be such to the older man. With more than a little chagrin, he did as told but refused to undress. He wanted no excuses for his nurse to stay away.

Chapter 8

Mouth set in a grim line, Camille held the spoonful of broth to her patient's lips. The corners of his mouth twitched, and she knew he was trying not to laugh. It only made her all the more furious with the task at hand.

She was about to pull away when he parted his lips. As he slowly and quite seductively accepted the offered spoon, she found herself mesmerized. Her own lips suddenly quaked with yearning for even the merest touch of his.

He cleared his throat, breaking his spell on her, and she nervously withdrew the spoon. She felt furious at herself for letting her guard slip. No matter what he might say or do, he was the cause for her predicament, and she would do well to remember that.

With the bowl of broth now empty, she stood to leave but didn't make it to the door.

"Miss du Carte," Reece said. "May I trouble you for some water? The broth was a bit salty."

Her shoulders tensed, and she gritted her teeth. After taking a deep breath, she poured him a glass of water from the pitcher on the nightstand and held it out to him. He looked up at her with all the weariness he could muster.

"I feel so weak," he whispered.

Knowing he played her for a fool, she managed to keep calm. Camille slipped her hand behind his back and helped him sit up. Holding the glass to his mouth, she let him drink his fill. Then, she deliberately tipped her hand so that enough water splashed onto his lap. Forcing down her own satisfied smile, she duly noted the shocked expression on his face.

"Why, sir," she exclaimed. "How clumsy of me. I do so apologize."

The game now afoot, he simply threw back the covers, revealing that he wore nothing but his underclothes. Camille inhaled sharply. Since he had a pajama top on, she had assumed that he was completely dressed. As she hurried out of the room, Reece found he could not hold back. His deep laughter chased her down the stairs.

* * * *

"Mother, might I ask how Miss du Carte has come to be under your roof?"

Mrs. Beauregard sighed. "She has been labeled a thief, Aristodemus."

Reece refused to let his face show his shock. His stomach knotted in sudden apprehension. "What did she steal?"

She frowned. "The only thing I know is that it was a bit of jewelry."

Reece paled, remembering the day he placed the ruby earrings in Camille's hand. His brows furrowed as he tried to remember what he had done with the receipt. He had thought it odd at the time that he had two receipts instead of one. He had meant to return it to Waldhorn's but had never gotten the chance.

He looked ruefully at his mother. "Come, now, since when have you ever not known the story of our resident convict's indictment?"

She eyed her son ruefully before relaying the events that led to Camille's capture. Apparently, the girl had been involved with a group of unnamed girls who had made a game of stealing. Camille was caught when she tried to have a pair of stolen earrings repaired at the same store she took them from. Mr. Waldhorn himself was there at the time, and she was arrested immediately.

A ball of acid formed in the pit of his stomach. Reece then knew that the jewelry had to have been the ruby earrings. As his mother straightened his room, he brooded on the information. He should come forward and help her. He knew that, but for some reason, he was reluctant to do so. He wanted her, and he knew she wasn't a thief. However, he wisely knew that she must blame him entirely for her current situation.

A plan formed in his head. One that would ensure the future of a certain convict, though he was sure she would never accept it. With good reason, she hated him, but somehow he would change that and in such a way that she would be unable to resist.

* * * *

Later that evening, Camille pushed open the bedroom door, tray in hand. She looked first at Fran, then at the arrogant man on the bed. Thrusting her chin up, she set the tray on his bedside table. With a hint of anger in her voice, she said, "I think we both know you are well enough to feed yourself."

"Aye, miss, but," Reece paused as he straightened out the fresh bed sheets across his lap. "Would you be so kind as to at least hand me the bowl?"

Noting it was indeed out of reach, she quickly handed it to him and turned to tend to Fran. His next words caused her to stop dead.

"I am sorry for all the trouble I have caused you, Miss du Carte."

She spun around. "Trouble? Oh, 'tis no trouble, sir. The

fact that my reputation has been destroyed. Nay, that is no trouble. The fact that no respectable man shall have me now, that is no trouble. Why, sir, I should thank you for ridding me of the trouble high society can be."

A bit taken aback, Reece quietly replied, "I meant the trouble of caring for me."

Though his face looked innocent enough, there was something hidden within the depths of his eyes to make Camille feel he knew exactly how she had arrived at his home. Yet, he played dumb. Her face drained. He had no intention of helping her.

Camille opened and closed her mouth several times as his words sunk in. Her eyes watered, and her chin lifted. "I think Fran needs me."

Turning sharply on her heel, she went to Fran's bedside as quickly as possible. Yet, no matter how much she tried to ignore him, Reece's eyes burned a hole in her back.

Chapter 9

It was a week before Thanksgiving, and Camille's heart surged with joy. Only a few more weeks, and she would be back home. She dearly missed her family. She had been allowed to use the telephone once a week to call. It was a most blessed privilege, and she was forever grateful for Mrs. Beauregard's kindness.

She paused from sweeping the parlor as muffled voices drew her attention to the porch. She stepped closer to the French doors. Reece sat on the swing as his mother fussed over him.

"Mother, I do not need a blanket," he protested.

Though Mrs. Beauregard's back was to her, Camille knew her eyes would be squinting dangerously. "Reece, it is too cold out here. I insist."

"No," he growled.

"Aristodemus!"

Camille watched the battle of wills, knowing who would win. She could not help but grin as Reece snatched the blanket out of his mother's hands. The two of them were so much alike, yet neither realized it. They both tried to be stern but tenderness more often than not reared its ugly head. Camille recalled how a few days ago Annie had brought a hurt kitten to Reece. He had immediately assisted her and had set up a makeshift cast on the poor thing's broken leg.

Mrs. Beauregard cleared her throat, and Camille jumped, chagrined at being caught staring at Reece. "He is asking that you bring him some hot tea."

Camille nodded, her cheeks flaming red, and hurried to do as she was bidden.

"Thank you, Miss du Carte," Reece said, gratefully accepting the warm mug. She took a step toward the door. "Please stay."

Her head snapped around, and gray eyes focused on his face. Darkness swirled in their depths, and Reece waited in anticipation for a spiteful response. He was, however, disappointed as she dipped her head and stared at the floor. Her fingers worried the gray material of her dress.

Sliding to the left, he patted the spot beside him. "Please sit."

Camille glanced at the empty spot and chose instead the iron loveseat. Reece smiled, and before she could protest, he claimed the vacant side.

"I believe you are right, Miss du Carte."

Camille looked at him with storm-colored eyes. Her voice was colder than the weather. "As to what, Mr. Duponte?"

"The wind blows less on this side of the porch."

She bit back a sharp retort. Had the loveseat allowed, she would have put space between them. As it was, their thighs touched, igniting something in her that she was trying desperately to squash.

Reece watched her every reaction, knowing she felt the powerful attraction between them. "Annie tells me you play the piano beautifully."

"I play, sir."

"I would love to hear you."

Camille started to rise, intent on his request. His hand reached out and blocked her attempt. "But not now."

Camille huffed and sat back. She looked to the door, half praying that Mrs. Beauregard would appear with a task for her to complete. The silence between them grew, and all Camille could think of was a pair of ruby earrings. Her breath caught in her throat, and her head swam.

"You could at least step forward and clear my name," she whispered through clenched teeth.

A strong urge to protect this lady's honor rose to the surface, but Reece pushed his chivalry down. He thought briefly of the receipts hidden in his dresser upstairs. Part of him was reluctant to give them up, even though he knew she was only going to be with them for a few more weeks.

He spoke his next words softly so that only she could hear. "Even if I were to step forward, what proof do I have? It is our word against theirs."

Triumph flashed across her face. "I knew you knew what I was talking about. How can you not help me?"

Her passionate response only enhanced her facial features, and Reece felt compelled to lean forward and kiss her. Camille tried to pull away, but he had slipped his arm around her back and held her close to him.

He traced the outline of her lips with his tongue, and the ice around her mouth began to melt. He continued his assault on her until her lips parted, allowing him entry to her soul. Memories of a certain dream flooded over her. The heat of her anger scattered in the cold winter air as she succumbed to his tender affections.

The slamming of the porch door caused them to pull apart guiltily. The two looked into the face of Mrs. Beauregard. Yet her face was neither angry nor disapproving.

"Camille, would you please bring Fran her dinner?"

As Camille scrambled to obey, Mrs. Beauregard flashed Reece a reproachful look.

* * * *

Camille stood on the south side of the front porch, looking to the woods where Reece had entered. Despite his mother's objections, Reece had gone off to make an evening hunt. He had asked Camille to join him, but before she could even protest, Mrs. Beauregard had firmly denied him.

Now, on retrospect, she secretly wished she had been allowed. The walls seemed to be closing in on her, and she wondered if a small adventure would cure her restlessness. Ever since that kiss, she had been as jumpy as a cat.

Sighing, Camille realized she had been daydreaming and turned to resume sweeping the porch. She nearly jumped out of her skin to find Reece standing quietly behind her. He grinned, put two fingers to his lips and beckoned her to follow him. She hesitated with a reproachful look in her eyes.

"I have a surprise for you," he whispered, taking her hand and pulling her toward the woods on the north side. "But we must be quiet."

As Camille glanced around nervously for Mrs. Beauregard, Reece patted her hand comfortingly. "We shant be long, love."

A short time later, the two were well into the cold, silent woods. She followed blindly behind him, wondering why she was allowing the cad to take her off like this. Of course, her hand was still clamped firmly in his warm masculine one. It suddenly struck her as odd that his hand felt smooth. She had assumed a sailor's hands would be rough and callused.

They stopped before a large oak tree and only then did Reece let go of her hand. To the left of the tree was a thicket of bushes, and Reece knelt before them. He looked over his shoulder at her and smiled in pure boyish abandonment. Upon his gesture, she knelt beside him as quietly as possible. When he pushed some of the brush aside, she gasped.

A nest of baby rabbits wiggled and squirmed before them. Reece reached in and gently picked up one and placed it in Camille's hand. Nervously, she looked around for the mother.

"Careful, love, they're delicate," Reece whispered.

"Where is his mother? Did she abandon them?"

Reece shook his head. "No, she only comes to the nest twice a day—once in the morning and once in the evening."

Using her finger, Camille petted the gray bunny. A thought suddenly occurred to her, and she raised frantic eyes to Reece's face. "'Tis certain she will abandon him now that we have touched him."

Reece shook his head again. "Trust me, love. She won't be that concerned."

Instantly comforted, Camille turned her attention back to the baby. Reece knew the woods much better than herself. Thus, she mentally pushed aside her concerns and concentrated on the treasure she held.

Reece and Camille were so close their heads nearly touched, and once again, she became acutely aware of him. Her first instinct was to bolt, but the baby in her hands caused her to stay put. She swallowed over a lump in her throat and looked into his violet-blue eyes. She instantly realized she had made a mistake, for she became lost in the spell enveloping them.

Before she could object, he captured her lips with his own. Slipping an arm behind her back, he pulled her close. When the baby rabbit mewed, he pulled away, smiled and put the baby back in its nest. Then, before she could escape, he pulled her to him and resumed the kiss.

Twisting their bodies around, Reece laid her gently on the ground and leaned over her. His eyes noted the lovely

flush in her cheeks and the way her lips were parted in anticipation. Her breath came in small gasps, further igniting the
fire in his loins.

"Why can't I get you out of my head?" he whispered, before crushing his lips to hers.

With a will of their own, her hands found their way
around his neck and into the softness of his hair. *Why indeed,*
she wondered, lost in his gentle affections.

Closing her eyes, she reveled in the kisses he rained upon
her face and neck. She felt as if she were floating on a cloud,
and she clung to his broad shoulders as if her very life de-
pended on it.

Reluctantly, he pulled back and simply stared at her. Desire swirled in his eyes, darkening the violet to a deep purple.
He cupped her cheek with the palm of his hand and rubbed his
thumb over her plump lips. He sighed.

"I think someone has stolen my heart."

Camille's eyes widened in surprise. "What are you saying?"

A tender smile touched the corners of his mouth. "I'm
saying that I'm in love with you."

A warning screamed in her head, and she scooted out
from beneath him. Jumping to her feet, she crossed her arms
and backed away from him.

"If you love me, then why won't you help clear my
name?" she cried softly. Her voice cracked with torment.

Taken off guard, Reece merely gaped at her. His loss of
words sent her into a rage. She turned on her heel and raced
off in the opposite direction before he could get to his feet. Instead of chasing her, however, he simply leaned against a tree
and waited. The path she had chosen would dead end shortly,
and she would be forced to return.

Minutes later, the sound of her screams had him running.

His heart caught in his throat at the sight of a huge wild dog attached to her right arm. Blood covered her, and Reece went insane.

Grabbing the nearest broken tree limb, he blindly attacked the dog. The instant the thick branch made contact, the dog let go of Camille and turned on Reece. Having the upper hand, however, he slammed the limb against the beast's head. The dog took one step and crumpled in an unconscious heap.

Reece then turned to Camille, who sat on the ground. She watched him through shock filled eyes, cradling her damaged hand against her body. Her face was tear stained, and her hair was in complete disarray. He gently picked her up and carried her home.

* * * *

Still in shock, Camille allowed Mrs. Beauregard to tuck the covers around her. She sat in the bed with her back up against the headboard, cradling her bandaged arm. Her eyes were glazed as she became lost once again in painful memory.

Reece leaned in the doorway, watching his mother fuss over her charge. His brows drew together, and his muscles tensed at the thought of the wild dog. He knew he would react the same way if he had to do it all over again.

His mother faced him and quietly motioned him into the next room, out of Camille's hearing. He braced for a scolding.

"The doctor's worried about rabies," she whispered.

His eyes widened, and his heart stopped briefly. "No."

"He gave her a shot of Pasteur's new wonder drug for rabies, and he left enough for one shot each day for the next thirteen days."

Reece nodded. "I have heard of it. It's quite effective from what I understand."

"Reece!"

Camille's voice had him practically running to her side. He knelt beside the bed as she grabbed his hands. Her eyes were moist with unshed tears.

"What's wrong?"

"I'm sorry. It's just..." She dipped her head in embarrassment.

"What?"

"I was frightened. 'Tis irrational, I know."

Reece cupped her cheek with his hand, and she closed her eyes, luxuriating in his gentle touch. Sleep tugged at her as the laudanum did its job.

"Stay with me 'til I fall asleep," she pleaded.

The concern on his face washed away with her simple request. "Aye, love, I will."

Hours later, Reece woke with a start. He had fallen asleep beside the bed, and he realized he still held her hand.

* * * *

The next night, as Camille lay in bed, the thought occurred to her that Reece had risked his life for her. A strange warmth surged through her heart, giving her more cause to wonder.

Chapter 10

"I've invited the Marchand's for Thanksgiving dinner," Mrs. Beauregard stated, never looking up from her knitting.

Both Reece and Annie rose their heads to gape at her. Then they looked at one another in absolute horror. Each stifled a groan.

"I feel it is only right as they put Annie and Clive up whilst Yellow Jack ran amuck in our household."

Annie was about to protest, but Reece shot her a warning glance and shook his head. She sighed and tried to focus her attention on the chessboard between them. She absolutely, positively, could not stand Penelope Marchand. Thanksgiving would be a disaster.

Seated beside Annie on the couch, Camille's curiosity was piqued as she watched the siblings' reactions. She wondered what the Marchand's had done to deserve such a reaction. She resolved to remain positive and not let others cloud her judgment of people she had never met.

"Will you join us as well, Camille?"

Alarm ran through her. "Oh, Mrs. Beauregard, I couldn't. You've shown me too many liberties as it is. The other servants—"

"I don't give a hoot what the other servants think," Mrs. Beauregard stated, her eyes flashing angrily. "You will join us, and that is that."

"I'll save you a seat," Reece whispered, a twinkle of mischief in his eyes.

Trapped, all Camille could do was accept. "Thank you, Mrs. Beauregard. I'd be delighted."

* * * *

Taking a deep breath, Camille smoothed down the skirts of her dress. On a whim, her mama had packed one simple brown dress. She was grateful as she did not want to wear one of her 'prison' dresses with company present.

Lifting her chin, she stepped into the dining room. Her eyes instantly locked with Reece's. He quickly rushed to her side and grabbed her hand.

"Mr. and Mrs. Marchand," he said. "May I introduce Miss Camille du Carte."

Camille held her breath as she watched the mixture of emotions cross the woman's face, noting that she was quick to compose herself. Whatever the woman's feelings, the mask that she now wore hid them well.

"It is a pleasure to meet you," the blonde haired beauty smiled.

The brown haired gentleman rose smoothly to his feet. Warning bells rang in her head as he took her in from head to toe. Reece's grip on her hand tightened, and she glanced briefly at him in consternation.

"Yes, I agree. I am delighted to make your acquaintance."

Mr. Marchand's voice was smooth as wine. Camille became uncomfortable under his stare. Allowing Reece to take charge, she let him lead her to a chair. She found herself between Reece and a young girl of about fourteen, who was giving her rather icy looks.

"Are you related to Clay du Carte?" Mr. Marchand asked.

Her face brightened. "Why, yes, sir. He is my father."

The man nodded. "I thought as much. He and I have faced one another aplenty in the courtroom."

"My husband practices mostly in Baton Rouge," the pretty blonde stated. "I find, however, that I prefer our lovely country side to that of city life."

"We have a town home in Baton Rouge, where I reside throughout the week," said Mr. Marchand.

"That's quite a commute, sir," Camille responded.

He tilted his head roguishly, toying with his long mustache. "I don't mind."

Camille quickly came to the conclusion that the man was a flirt. She had come across many such men at home. *No wonder his wife acts so queer. She knows of his roving eye.'*

"Is it time?" Annie asked. "May I say the blessing now?"

"By all means," her father stated.

Everyone bowed their heads as the prayer commenced. Annie's young voice echoed through the room. "Come, dear Jesus, be our guest. May this food be blessed, Amen. Oh, wait," Annie added. "I also want to ask that you bless those less fortunate than we are, and all the animals and especially my kitten. Amen."

"Amen," Camille whispered, a smile twitching at the corners of her mouth.

When she raised her head from prayer, the weight of a stare caused her to look to her left. Penelope's cold green eyes glared at her, but the child's smile was sweet. Purposefully, the girl bowed her head once more in prayer.

"Yes, dear Lord, bless all those convicts less fortunate than I. Amen."

Camille's face grew warm with embarrassment. Lifting her chin, she valiantly ignored the remark and pushed the hurt down. The entire room became quiet as Penelope's words sunk in.

Annie broke the silence. "You mean spirited little snippet," she hissed.

"Annie," warned Mrs. Beauregard.

Mindful of her mother, Annie clamped her mouth shut and resisted the urge to kick Penelope. She did, however, manage to throw several eye-daggers in Penelope's direction, though the fourteen year old was too busy mooning over Reece to notice.

Mr. Beauregard took over the conversation and turned the focus on matters other than Camille's household status. Thus, the rest of the meal was quite pleasant, despite Penelope's attempts to ambush Camille.

An overturned salt dispenser on her plate was handled with smiles and politeness. Even the spilled tea on her dress made Camille only that much more determined to shower the little princess with the utmost hospitality. Yet, she was never more relieved when dinner was over, and she was allowed to escape.

* * * *

Camille watched Annie explore the bed of late blooming flowers. The garden was slowly losing its life to winter, and Camille sighed despondently. She sat down on one of the white iron benches and soon lost herself in thoughts of home. A single tear slipped down her cheek. She could almost smell the smoke from one of her father's cigars.

She pictured everyone at the dinner table. Her papa would, as usual, be at the head of the table with her mama to his right. Catrina and her husband would be on the left. Uncle Robert would be seated at the opposite end of the table, and of course, her chair would be vacant.

Unless they invited someone to fill the empty spot. She sniffed. Her heart grew heavier at the thought.

A white handkerchief suddenly appeared in front of her

face. She looked up into violet-blue eyes. "I must apologize on my young neighbor's behalf."

Reece sat beside her and gently dabbed at the tears on her face. Then he held her chin with his fingertips, inspecting his handiwork. "Do not let Penelope bother you so."

"Oh no," Camille protested, shaking her head. "'Twas not her. It's just, well, I miss my family."

Reece nodded in understanding. "I know that feeling quite well."

"Yes, I suppose you do, what with all your traveling."

Somehow, his hand had found its way around hers, and she found its warmth comforting. Her heart sped up, and she forced herself to stare at the ground. Yet when his hand touched her cheek, she willingly fell into the fire of his eyes. He tilted his head, and the warmth of his lips melted her insides. Her eyes closed as she savored the moment.

Then, one dirty little word flew into her head, and a thin layer of ice surrounded her heart. *Earrings.*

She pulled back, placing her free hand on his chest. The ice in her heart matched her voice. "Don't."

"Why?" His voice was deep with passion. "'Tis just a kiss. I ask for nothing more."

Her eyes narrowed. "You know what stands between us."

"What good would it do anyway? The damage has been done."

As regally as possible, Camille rose to her feet, tossing her next words in the air as she walked away. "Aye, sir, the damage has been done. My reputation is lost, and this…whatever it is between us can never be."

Chapter 11

The first gift that appeared on Camille's bed was a piece of mistletoe. Her cheeks flamed red at its apparent innuendo and tossed it on the floor. Her temper rose, and she slammed things about as she got ready for bed. It took hours that night before sleep visited.

After that, gifts appeared regularly on her pillow, ranging from chocolate candy and books to sheet music for the piano. At first, she was tempted to destroy every last one, but common sense and practicality prevailed.

Thus, the chocolate was eaten with great delight. The books were perused with great care, and the sheet music was learnt the very next day. All of this, of course, after her chores were completed.

Reece, however, made himself scarce, never letting on that he was the giver. If he entered a room that she was in, he would exchange civilities with her and make a hasty retreat. His mother had been quite insistent that her charge remain unsullied and had given Reece the motherly look, which said she knew exactly where his thoughts had been headed. Therefore, in compliance with rules set by society, he began his subtle courtship.

* * * *

Christmas Eve had at last arrived and was at an end. After

assisting with the serving of dinner, Camille had been allowed to return to her room. She closed the door, thankful that Mrs. Beauregard trusted her enough to leave it unlocked. She had no thoughts of running away and jeopardizing her term of service. The sooner she got home the better.

She leaned against the door, grateful to escape Reece's heated eyes. His gaze had followed her as she had moved about the dining room, and she felt like everyone knew. Of course, she was being silly. Annie's excitement in regard to St. Nicholas had dominated the dinner conversation.

Closing her eyes, she fancied that she still heard the piano dancing with Christmas music. Reece and Annie had taken turns entertaining, and Camille had hid in the shadows, thankful they did not ask her to join. Just watching him caused her heart to speed up, and when their eyes had met from across the room, it was a wonder her dress didn't burst into flames. She had a moment's feeling of shame for her wantonness.

Sighing, she turned to get ready for bed, and a startled cry escaped her lips. Spread out across the bed was a stunning emerald dress with matching shoes. Her hand flew to her throat, and tears filled her eyes. The note simply stated she was to wear it on Christmas day. A knock at the door made her jump, and she hurried to answer it, feeling guilty for some reason.

"It was not entirely his idea," Mrs. Beauregard smiled. She looked past Camille at the dress on the bed. Then she took her by the shoulders and looked her straight in the eye. "You are by far the most amenable of my charges. Thus, I have allowed you liberties the others did not deserve."

"Thank you," Camille whispered.

"We have never discussed the reason why you are here."

Camille's high spirits sunk at the mention of it. Her chin dipped briefly before she jerked it up. She refused to let herself feel bad for something she did not do. Before she could stop herself, the words escaped her lips.

"I am innocent," she whispered.

Mrs. Beauregard honored her with a sad smile. "I know."

Camille's eyes watered, and her throat dried up. She swallowed nervously. Mrs. Beauregard stepped back. "Wear the dress, Camille. Please."

* * * *

She sighed, luxuriating in the feel of silk against her skin. It had been six months of wearing only cotton. The dress fit perfectly as well as the shoes, and she wondered where and when they had gotten what she termed her Christmas present.

A bit nervous, Camille stepped into the doorway of the parlor. The Beauregard family was immersed in Christmas gaieties. As such, she was able to watch them as they opened their presents. For the briefest of moments, her heart lurched as she thought of her own family opening their gifts without her. She deftly pushed the troublesome thought aside, realizing how adept she was becoming at that.

"Oh, Camille."

Annie's squeal of admiration completely brought her back to the room. Warmth rushed to her cheeks as she realized they were all staring at her, especially Reece. The look on his face caused the heat to extend to her neck and bosom.

"It seems we are quite fortunate, Reece," Mr. Beauregard's deep voice boomed across the room.

"In what respect, sir?" Reece found himself unable to take his eyes off Camille.

"Why, the presence of such lovely female companions, what else?"

As Camille took a seat beside Mrs. Beauregard, a knock sounded loudly on the front door. Her attention was focused on Annie as the girl showed off her presents. Thus, she did not notice the conspiratorial look between Mr. and Mrs. Beauregard.

A shadow fell in the doorway, and when the silence deepened, Camille felt obligated to look. Her eyes filled with joyous tears, and her hands flew to her mouth. In childlike abandon, she jumped to her feet and raced to where her parents stood and threw her arms around her MaMa.

It felt so good to hold her mother; she didn't want to let go. Camille hadn't realized how much she missed the warmth of her embrace. She breathed in the scent of her mother's favorite perfume, closing her eyes as she thought of distant memories.

The fatherly embrace was brief but comforting. She looked up into her father's face through the tears in her eyes. She placed her right hand on his smooth cheek and laughed.

"So she finally got you to shave that nasty beard."

Clay smiled in response. "Let's just say it was one of her Christmas presents."

Camille glanced at her mother before facing the room of Beauregards. She looked directly at Mrs. Beauregard and smiled. "Thank you."

Mrs. Beauregard shook her head and looked at her husband, who simultaneously cleared his throat. Astonished, Camille gracefully approached him and placed a demure kiss on his cheek.

"Thank you," she repeated, stepping back.

The next half-hour was spent making small pleasantries. Annie played with her toys while the adults conversed. Reece kept his distance from Camille, but not his gaze.

When his mother suggested they let Camille and her parents have some personal time, Reece politely objected. Stepping away from his perch against the wall, he nervously cleared his throat.

"I have a present for Camille."

Reaching into his coat pocket, he pulled out a small package and handed it to her. Then he waited while his heart hammered painfully in his chest.

Almost fearfully, Camille unwrapped the package. Her hands stilled as she stared at the blue-velvet jewelry box. The blood pounded in her ears. *This better not be a pair of ruby earrings,* she thought as she angrily flipped open the box.

Her anger turned to astonishment as she viewed a solitary white diamond ring. Panic rose within her, and her eyes darted to Reece's absurdly humble face. *If I didn't know any better,* she thought.*'Twould seem to be—*

"An engagement ring. Oh my." Her mother's voice interrupted her thoughts.

Reece quickly jumped to an explanation. "Yes, ma'am. I apologize, Mr. du Carte, for not approaching you first, but there had been no adequate opportunity last night at the inn."

The room remained speechless as Camille continued to stare at the ring. Then, as eloquently as possible, she rose to her feet. The snapping shut of the box's lid bounced off the walls. The distance between them closed within seconds. With as much restraint as possible, she held it out to him.

"I daresay I hope you kept the receipt this time," she growled. "I am afraid I cannot accept."

* * * *

Hope du Carte locked eyes with her husband before following their daughter out onto the porch. The girl paced back and forth, obviously irritated by the recent event in the parlor. Used to her daughter's temper, she wondered what the young man had done to set off such an adamant refusal.

"Camille, darling." She stepped into the path of pacing and caught her by the shoulders. "Why did you refuse? In light of recent events, you should be more than willing to accept such a gracious offer."

The storm clouds in her eyes turned deathly dark. "You

have no idea what you are talking about, Mother, and as for your so-called perfect match, he is a lying scoundrel who has no clue as to how to treat a lady, much less defend her honor."

"Well, obviously they have come to accept you here," her mother stated, sweeping her hand around. "You have been allowed privileges I know most convicted felons would never have been allowed."

Her mouth dropped at her mother's forthrightedness. The blush on her cheeks deepened as her mother continued her lecture. "Society can be vicious, Camille. Do not think you will just waltz back into the community with no one the wiser. I am afraid the rumors about you have become well stretched beyond the truth. Why, I have even heard that you are in league with pirates, of all the absurd things."

Aye, he could well be defined as a pirate, Camille thought. She crossed her arms and thrust up her chin. "I will not marry him."

The closing door drew her attention to her father's entrance onto the porch. He had one of his awful cigars and proceeded to light it. He puffed on the wretched thing before joining the conversation. "Camille, it is my opinion that you're mother is right on this account. At least take it into consideration."

He drew on the cigar and let out a trail of smoke. "I have already discussed it with young Reece and his parents. They are really quite fond of you, by the by."

Refusing to let him change the subject, she glared at him. "Just what did you discuss?"

"You will return home for one month. The Beauregard's have arranged for your early release, due to good behavior. We leave on the morrow."

"What happens after one month?"

"You will either accept young Reece's offer or enter a boarding school."

Chapter 12

December 31, 1889
New Orleans

Camille looked smugly about the room, absolutely sure that both her MaMa and PaPa had been wrong about society, about her friends. Not long after her return, Maggie's New Years Eve invitation had arrived on her doorstep, and now she stood on the threshold of what she hoped was a positive new beginning.

Maggie rushed to her side, with Emily not far behind. Her hands were taken in comrade fashion, and the customary hug ensued. Maggie, however, was unable to meet Camille's eyes and let Emily take over with a bit of relief.

"Dear, dear Camie," Emily cooed as she gave the briefest of hugs. Then she stepped back, holding out her hands as if she had plunged them in dirty water. As Emily wiped her hands on the towel offered by the nearby servant, Camille's eyes narrowed.

She lost the opportunity of a nasty response as the entrance of Brent Lafourche and his entourage distracted Emily. A bit guiltily, Maggie barely glanced at Camille as they brushed past her to greet the young men. Feeling a chill in the room, Camille turned to stop Maggie, only to find an unexpected display of affection between her best friend and her ex-beau.

Shocked, Camille gulped, and her hand immediately went to the cross at her neck, pulling strength from it. She took two steps back before her eyes met Emily's satisfied glower. Thrusting her chin up, Camille turned back to the room full of young and old alike. There were plenty others with whom to hold a conversation with. She turned on her heel and fled into the safety of the crowd.

* * * *

Punch in hand, Camille froze beside the open doorway. Voices had stopped her from entering the room. More precisely, it had been the mention of her name that had given her pause.

"Unbelievable."

"Amazing is a more appropriate word. I'm surprised the little convict had the nerve to actually show her face." Emily's voice caused icy fingernails to dance across Camille's skin. The next voice, however, caused her heart to burst into shreds.

"I have it on good word, mind you, that the plantation owner's son actually plied for her hand. I can see the invitation now. Mr. and Mrs. du Carte and Mr. and Mrs. Beauregard request the presence of your company at the wedding of Convict Camille to Country Bumpkin," Maggie said and giggled.

Tears sprang to her eyes at the realization that her parents were right. They had only invited her out of perverse curiosity. Her hands shaking, she sloshed punch on her brand new dress as she backed up to avoid discovery. The presence of a body behind her caused her to stop her silent retreat. She looked over her shoulder into violet-blue eyes.

Reece fluidly took the glass from her and slipped his hand

under her elbow. He tipped his head with a bit of a smile. "Country Bumpkin, at your service."

Camille could not suppress a smile. Strangely, the pain in her heart disappeared at the sight of him. "You heard."

"Shall we give them a show, my love?"

Her gray eyes turned stormy. "Don't call me that."

He held his free hand up. "As you wish."

Camille found herself gently pulled into the room full of alligators. Reece tucked her hand firmly in his as all eyes turned their way. He smiled charmingly at them.

"Well, Camille, introduce me to your..." he hesitated, sending an icy stare Emily's way. "Friends."

Her lips were frozen as a wide mixture of emotions ran rampant through her. Reece patted her hand in understanding. "Allow me to introduce myself, as it seems a cat has stolen her tongue." He gave a slight inclination of his head. "Aristodemus Duponte, Camille's fiancé."

The group simultaneously dropped their jaws. Although she admitted to herself that it felt good to watch their reaction, sheer force of will kept her own mouth from falling open. It was all she could do to keep her temper at bay as the rest of the evening was spent satisfying the cats who had indeed stolen her tongue.

* * * *

As the clock chimed the arrival of 1890, Reece pulled Camille into a shadowed corner. His lips quickly stopped her protest, and the strength of his arms kept her from flight. She suffered the torture of his kiss, only to find her body betrayed her as surely as her ex-best friend had.

Warmth flooded over her as she relaxed against him. Her arms entwined around his neck, and her breasts pressed against the hard muscles in his chest. His sweet invasion of her mouth, however, lasted only seconds. She gasped for breath when he pulled away.

"Happy New Year, Camille." His voice sent desire shuddering through her.

Amazed at her own reaction, she ceased to think as she stared up into his handsome face. She swallowed before reality rushed in. Then she quickly tried to cover up her response with conversation.

"So how were you able to receive an invite?" she whispered.

His violet-blue eyes danced mischievously. "Who said I was invited?"

"Then how did you know there was a party and where it was?"

"I have.my ways."

Camille looked dubiously at him. "Really, now?"

"Really." He hesitated before adding. "I do recall quite a bit of mail from a certain Maggie Lafitte."

She softened her barrage of questions. "Her return address. Very clever, Mr. Duponte."

"Thank you, Miss du Carte."

Her storm-filled eyes narrowed. "And I don't suppose a set of parents had anything to do with it."

He played the shocked role of a discovered spy quite well. "I guess I am not so clever as one would think."

"Aye, 'twould seem so," she smiled.

His eyes blazed with heat, and she felt herself drawn deeper into his spell. The room and all its occupants disappeared, leaving only them. Camille tried her best to think of something to say, but he won.

"Did you like the books?

She nodded. "Yes, thank you."

"And the dress?"

"'Twas beautiful, thank you."

"Yet you did not find this to your liking?"

Camille looked down at his hand. In his palm sat the blue jewelry box, opened to reveal the modest diamond ring. Before she could open her mouth to protest, she saw that his attention was focused on something over her shoulder. Resisting the urge to look, she reluctantly slipped the ring out of the box and onto her finger.

"Make note, you scoundrel," she whispered. "This is not my answer. I have yet to be convinced of the likes of you."

Reece merely smiled before acknowledging the couple a few feet behind them. "Happy New Year, Mr. Lafourche."

Camille's eyes grew wide, and her back went ramrod stiff. With all the grace she could muster, she masked her face in a smile and turned to face her ex-beau.

"Why, Brent, it is *so* very good to see you," she said, fighting the urge to grind her teeth. Maggie was on his arm.

"Happy New Year," the pale girl whispered.

"Show her your ring, love," Reece whispered as he slipped his arms around her waist from behind.

Fighting the urge to scowl, Camille held out her hand, allowing her ex-best friend to inspect the beautiful diamond. Maggie's hand felt cool and somewhat clammy. Then, after the required 'oo-ing' and 'ah-ing,' Maggie held up her own left hand for observation.

A big, beautiful heart-shaped diamond sparkled atop her finger. Camille's eyes grew wide at the size of it, instantly wondering how Brent was able to afford such a gem. While his father had considerable wealth, Brent was still attending Tulane University and had yet to enter law school. Somewhere in the back of her head, warning signals clanged at full attention, but she was unable to contemplate the information. Her parents chose that moment to walk up.

Goodbyes were exchanged, and Reece followed them out

of the house. Ever the gentleman, he took Camille's left hand and raised it to his lips. The diamond ring sparkled in the gas lamps that lit the street, inadvertently catching the eye of Mrs. du Carte. With a satisfied smile, she quietly noted the small step Reece had gained. Despite her previous doubts, the evening had proven a success.

Chapter 13

The following weeks found Camille's social calendar filled to the brim, and to her chagrin, Reece had also been invited to every event. Despite the fact that she was a felon, she found herself in the midst of Maggie and Emily's little group, although she could not figure out why. Nonetheless, it gave her the opportunity to observe them close up. She hoped that somehow one of them would slip up and confirm her suspicions.

Then came a golden opportunity. Maggie invited her to stay the night, along with Emily and one other girl. She forced her hands to quit shaking as she answered affirmative to the missive and sent it back via servant to Maggie. Then she sank into a nearby chair, her eyes sparkling with eager anticipation. She knew without a doubt that she was on the verge of discovery.

* * * *

Camille stared at the ceiling of Maggie's bedroom. Her eyes had finally become adjusted to the dark, and her ears strained for the telltale sounds of her companions' onset of deep slumber. Then, she quietly pushed back the covers and crept across the room to Maggie's desk.

Leaning over it, she reached behind it and carefully withdrew a small book from its hiding spot. Years ago, her friend had shown her where she hid her diary. Now Camille would use it to her advantage.

A loud sigh behind her caused her to freeze with the book in mid-air. Her heart slammed into her rib cage, and her breath caught in her throat. Once the danger of being caught passed, she quickly hid the diary in her suitcase and slipped back into bed. She knew when she got home, she would have a better chance to peruse the forbidden text. A moment of guilt gave her pause, but she shook the feeling off and forced herself to sleep.

Had she been able to see more clearly in the dark, Emily's coldly gleaming eyes would have sent her scurrying to slip the book back in its place.

* * * *

The next afternoon, Camille paced her room nervously. The diary lay shut on her bed, calling her with its mere presence. Long ago, Maggie had entrusted her with its hiding place. Now she was betraying her, and it was one of the hardest things she ever had to do.

With a frustrated sigh, she flopped on the bed, grabbed the book and flipped it open to the latest page. Her heart plummeted into her stomach at the single entry dated day before last.

I fear for my life.

Quickly skimming the previous pages, she saw nothing interesting until January 1, 1890.

She seems to always come out smelling like a rose. Her fiancée is so handsome. Her ring, however, is so small. Mine is so much better.

Camille's indignation rose to the surface. Without a moment's hesitation, the following thoughts flew through her head. *What care I of size when it was given in love?*

A second later, she almost dropped the book when she realized what had just occurred to her. *Could it possibly be love?*

She thought of how every time Reece entered a room, her heart jumped, and she couldn't take her eyes off him. She even found herself wondering what he was doing while they were apart. They had been together much during the last few weeks. Camille realized that she had let her guard slip, and he had somehow crept into her heart.

Swallowing over the lump in her throat, she continued to read Maggie's diary. The next entry further astounded her.

> *I wish Brent loved me as much as Reece loves Camille. Alas, would that I were so fortunate.*

Camille growled softly. *If he loves me so much, why doesn't he help prove my innocence? Or at least try?*

Shoving aside her emotions, she concentrated on the diary. She skimmed through pages, searching for entries before the date of her incarceration. The date of October 31, 1889 stopped her first.

> *I am torn between fear and love. The greatest thing has happened tonight, as well as something from my nightmares. We performed the ritual tonight. I should not speak of it, but I feel I must purge my soul within these pages. I daresay I cannot confess this to a priest. I pray God will accept this as my confessional.*
>
> *We performed it in the oldest part of the cemetery, near Marie Laveaou's grave. Brent had been frustrated when we discovered the Laveaou family standing guard by her grave. Apparently, they were used to this sort of thing happening on All Hallow's Eve. We therefore found a more secluded spot*

out of their hearing.

The three of us were donned all in black, and I was unable to see the faces of my accomplices. Brent's masculine voice whispered through the air as he chanted. I daresay, it sent a shiver of wantonness through me. Emily placed the bowl on the gravestone as we formed a triangle.

My hands shook as I withdrew the blood pouch. Brent had already taken care of the offertory blood. It was fresh, only an hour old. I dared not ask him how he acquired it nor if it were human or animal. Some things are best left unknown.

Upon Brent's indication, I carefully dumped the blood into the bowl and waited. I daresay I had no idea what to expect, whether an explosion or what, but when the owl in the tree beside us hooted, I nearly jumped out of my skin. We all did. I was ready to take flight, but the two of them gripped my hands tightly, as if reading my very thoughts.

After a moment of listening to the sounds of the night, Brent finally said that it was good. I was never so grateful and forced myself to walk beside them instead of running like my instincts screamed to.

Emily's house was the closest, so we saw her home first, and then Brent accompanied me to mine. As I leaned upon the back door, Brent pressed his body against mine. He pushed the hood from my head and tasted of my lips. It was divine. Then, to my astonishment, he dropped to his knees and held out a ring box. He asked me to marry him. I, of course, said that he would have to discuss it with my father, and if such was in agreeance, then I would be delighted. He seemed pleased with my answer, and I know he shall call upon father on the morrow.

My heart is filled with happiness.

Camille frowned, wondering why the three of them were meddling in the forbidden black arts. Was it connected to the thefts? Sighing, she rested her head on the diary and closed her eyes, letting her thoughts clear.

* * * *

"Camille."

The soft echo of her name caused Camille to lift her head. She found that she stood in the midst of a crowd made of fog. A cloud-made woman stepped before her, blocking her path. As she stared, the woman's face took solid shape, and vibrant colors came to life.

The Creole woman wore a Mardi Gras mask fashioned to represent a serpent. It covered her eyes and nose, and fangs hung over her upper lip. Her silver and black dress shined like a snake's skin and clung to every curve. Around her throat was a real snake that slithered over and around the woman's outstretched arms.

Without a moment's thought, Camille placed her hand in the woman's and watched in silent horror as the woman forced the snake's fangs to sink into Camille's wrist. Then, the snake-lady laughed and danced into the fog. Camille found her voice and sank to her knees screaming.

Warm strong hands grasped her shoulders, and she looked up into a face wearing a gold eye mask and top hat. She gasped and scrambled back from the figure. Her heart beat furiously.

Almost instantaneously, the figure quickly reached up and withdrew the mask. Camille felt immediately foolish as she realized it was Reece. Behind him stood her concerned mother. Confused, she looked about to see that she was on the floor beside her bed. Obviously, she had fallen asleep.

A bit embarrassed, she sat up. "I'm ok. Sorry. It was just a nightmare."

"Are you sure?"

Reece's deep voice helped pull her back to reality. She nodded as he helped her up." He frowned. "Perhaps we should not go to the ball tonight."

"Oh, no. I feel fine," she protested. She glanced at her mother, who already had on the black satin dress that went with her cat mask. "What time is it?"

"Time for young Reece to wait downstairs while I help you get ready for the Mardi Gras ball."

Chapter 14

Camille fanned herself with the butterfly fan that went with her costume. Despite the cooler temperature outside, the dance room was hot. She placed her hand beseechingly on Reece's arm.

"There are too many people. Might we go for some fresh air?"

Reece nodded. "Of course."

Within seconds, they stood upon the long balcony overlooking St. Charles Street. They leaned against the rail and watched the people walk by.

Reece cleared his throat. "I'm glad we have this opportunity alone."

He placed his hand over Camille's but continued his position by her side. "I realize I forced the ring upon you at the New Year's Eve party, and despite the fact that your parents have taken this as a yes on your part, I have not."

Camille's heart leapt into her throat, yet she kept her silence, anxious to hear what he had to say. His fingers pulled tightly around hers. He dropped his head and stared at his feet.

"I grow weary of this dance, Camille. I despise society, yet I have found myself thrown into the midst of it. I chose years ago to become a sailor to escape these bonds. Now I find myself right back where I started."

Violet-blue eyes suddenly focused on her face. "I am drawn to you. I can't seem to get enough of you. I go to bed each night wondering if you even think of me when we are apart, for I find that you are constantly on my mind. I don't even feel right when you are gone from my side."

Camille found herself drawn into the depths of his eyes. She licked her lips nervously, for the first time really noticing the magnetic force that drew her to him. Images of their outings over the last few weeks flew through her head. She found that she could not get enough of his laughter, and the way he moved had her hypnotized. He doted on her as if she were a princess, which made her eyes water at the thought.

His smile seemed sad as he wiped the tear that spilled from her eye. "I see. You haven't the heart to tell me."

Camille shook her head. "You misunderstand," she whispered. "For it was just today that my heart made itself known to me."

Reece's eyes glimmered with instant hope. He opened his mouth to speak, but she held up her hand.

"Hear me out, kind sir. My answer is yes, and not because you are my only chance out of this mess I find myself—" She hesitated, afraid to say out loud what she felt inside. The bubble in her heart expanded, though, and the words came unbidden but with great emotion.

"I find myself to be in love with you, sir."

Her chin lifted in defiance, daring him to laugh triumphantly at her. Indeed, he grinned but then crushed her to him in a rush of passion he could no longer deny. His lips found hers, and the world around them stilled.

When at last they drew apart, his eyes reflected what shone in her own. He smiled as unexpected happiness filled his heart. "I love you so, my dear Camille."

He wrapped his arms around her, and she laid her head on his chest. A sigh of relief escaped her lips, and she closed her eyes in contentment. As he spoke, she felt the deep timber of his voice rumble through his chest.

"I do not wish for a long engagement, my love. Six weeks, and you shall be mine."

Alarmed, she pulled away to look into his handsome face. "But that's too soon. They will think——"

His violet-blue eyes narrowed. "Society can go to Hell, Camille. When will you realize they can't make you happy?"

She bit her lower lip and nodded. "I suppose you are right."

She shivered as a breeze found its way between them. Though the sleeves on her dress covered her arms, the cold air suddenly had her chilled.

"You're cold. Wait here while I get your coat."

Camille nodded and leaned against the rail as Reece hurried inside. Though it was late, the people on the street below took no notice. Mardi Gras pushed aside normal conventions as revelry lasted late into the night. She herself had never been out this late before and stared in awe at the people's candor.

The whooping and hollering and display of affection between couples had her blushing behind her butterfly mask. She averted her eyes, briefly wondering where her parents were and why it was taking Reece so long to fetch her coat.

Suddenly, a pair of arms encircled her waist and pulled her into a warm embrace. She relaxed into it, closing her eyes to savor the heat. "Do you wish children, my love?" she asked.

"What a bold invitation, my butterfly."

Camille jumped and tried to pull away as she realized the man behind her was not Reece. Strong arms, however, held her firmly in place. "Let go, sir. It seems I have mistaken you for someone else."

"Ah, but I have not mistaken you, dear Camille. Once, long ago, it was my arms you sought out."

At that confession, Brent let her go, and she quickly stepped away. Turning to face him with a scathing remark, she found he had moved a ways down the balcony and smiled sweetly at her. "What would your new love think if he learned of the kisses you just gave me?"

Her fury rose swiftly. "But I gave you none."

"Ah, but he does not know that."

Brent disappeared around the corner, and Camille looked frantically at the open doors. There was still no sign of Reece. Brashly, she hurried after Brent.

When she rounded the corner, she ran right into him. Too shocked to do anything, she found herself locked in an unwanted embrace. Cold lips pressed against hers, and as his tongue sought entrance, she pushed ineffectively against his chest in an effort to get away. Her fight only ignited his desire.

Knowing the shadows hid them, he pushed her up against the wall, keeping his lips firm against her mouth to keep her from calling out. His free hand riffled through the folds of her dress, seeking the heat between her thighs. She grew frantic then, as terror rushed through her. She pulled at his hair and sank her nails into his neck, but it bothered him naught. Just as she thought all was lost, Brent was pulled away from her, and she sank weakly to the ground, trembling.

Caught off guard, Brent was unprepared for the unrelenting assault of a man gone insane with anger. Reece hit him in the face so hard that he fell against the wall, stunned. Reece was upon him in an instant, pummeling his face with brutal fists.

"You dare touch her again, and I will see you are alligator meat," Reece whispered menacingly in his opponent's ear. He pressed Brent's face into the building wall. "One word of this to anyone, and I will see your fiancée knows as well."

For good measure, Reece slammed Brent's head against the wall once more before letting him go. The man slid to the floor, all the fight beaten out of him. He'd never had a chance to gather any of his wits about him to even defend himself.

Reece knelt beside a shaken Camille. With eyes as wide as a doe, she gratefully accepted his helping hand. He pulled her tightly against him and quickly ushered her inside. As soon as they found her parents, they quickly took their shaken daughter home.

* * * *

Camille closed her eyes as the laudanum her mother had given quickly made her drowsy. She moved in and out of nightmares, and when the bed dipped beside her, she merely thought herself immersed in yet another.

She opened her eyes in time to see a cloth covering her face. Strong arms held her down when she began to struggle. The effects of the ether worked quickly with the laudanum already in her system, and she felt her limbs go limp. She had no control and felt as if she floated on air. She fought with her eyes to keep them open.

Her heart leapt in her throat at the sight of a skull mask looming over her. The man lifted her in his arms, his breath reeking of alcohol.

"Let's see how quickly you are saved this time, sweet Camille."

As her eyes rolled back in her head, she knew it was Brent.

* * * *

She woke to find her hands tied above her head and her feet tied wide apart. A filthy rag had been shoved against her mouth and tied in place to keep her from screaming. Over her face, an eyeless mask had been placed to keep her from seeing her abductor. Thankfully, she realized she was still clothed in her nightdress. Dampness, however, penetrated the thin material, and she realized she lay upon a cold, hard slab of some sort. A sharp inhale told of mold and decay, and she wondered where Brent had taken her.

Sensing movement around her, she struggled to make sense of what was happening. Soft chanting reached her ears, and it was then she realized that Brent had accomplices. Focusing on the voices, she knew without a doubt that one was Emily.

She pulled against her bonds, only to still instantly when a male hand pressed firmly against her womanhood. Her throat went dry as fingers touched where no man had ever been. A female voice squeaked through the air, giving name to the third person party to this nightmare.

"Brent, is that absolutely necessary?" Maggie cried in dismay.

"Yes," Brent replied coldly. "Our sacrifice must be pure in body, if not of soul."

The word 'sacrifice' sent alarm bells ringing wildly through Camille as she tried to comprehend what was happening to her. The drugs in her body still had their grip on her, and though she struggled, it was not for long. Wearily, she admitted rather reluctantly that she was caught fast in whatever diabolical scheme this threesome had in store for her.

Brent leaned close to her and whispered words in her ear. "I would like to take this moment to thank you for placing yourself in the hands of the law. They were close to catching us, but you threw them off our trail. My sincerest gratitude is yours, sweet Camille."

His rancid breath caused her stomach to churn, and she fought down the bile that rose in her throat. She refused to choke on her own vomit. Her thoughts turned elsewhere quickly as his hand crushed her right breast. She heard Maggie squeal in dismay. Brent ignored the outburst and continued his rough fondling.

"Seems a shame to waste such prime, untouched steak, but the Dios de la Abundancia decrees a virgin for his dinner, and you will not stand in the way of my fortune."

Camille swallowed as the tip of a knife dug lightly into her throat. The chanting resumed, although Maggie's voice quivered with the restraint of tears. Camille felt her own eyes go damp with the realization they meant to kill her.

Reece, where are you? she thought, as her heart ached.

"I promise it will be quick," Brent whispered in her ear. He straightened, speaking words of ritual. His hand pressed the blade firmly against her throat. She froze, wary of the fact that it would cut her if she moved an inch. Prayers filled her head as tears trickled down her face.

Please, dear God, don't let it end like this.

A horrible howling filled the room, causing the hairs on Camille's neck to rise. A deep voice then reverberated off the walls.

"Who dares disturb my rest?"

Emily and Maggie screamed, and if Camille had not been gagged, she would have also. Brent jumped, causing the knife to dig into Camille's flesh. Warm blood dripped down her neck.

"Maggie, Emily, wait, where are you going?" Brent cried.

A rush of cool air suddenly washed over Camille, and she realized the two girls had fled in fear, leaving only Brent. Unable to see, Camille felt rather than saw a presence on the left side of her. Her fear rose as wild images of ghostly beings danced in her head. As Brent was on her right, she could not fathom what type of being stood to her left.

A cold silence filled the room, and Camille strained to hear any sign of movement. It gave her time to realize she was trembling uncontrollably. Then Brent spoke, causing Camille to jump.

"Well, my good fellow, 'tis about time you showed yourself. Did you see the expression on their faces?" he laughed ominously. "The poor chits have no clue that they're being had. The only demon I bow to is money, and once I marry Maggie, I will have plenty of it, especially since her old man will shortly thereafter kick the bucket."

The other man made no reply, merely waiting for instructions from Brent. Camille moaned, tugging weakly at her bonds. Brent pulled the mask from her face and threw it aside. He placed a cold hand upon her cheek.

"Shhh, my dear," he whispered. "'Twill all be over soon, and you'll be on your way to some foreign country to learn the art of love in some lucky man's bed."

Camille stilled at the words as horror of the unknown swept through her. If not kill her, then apparently he meant to sell her into slavery. Thus, she would be out of the way, and Maggie and Emily would think he had killed her and disposed of her body. Her eyes narrowed, and she struggled once more against the rope that held her prisoner. Brent merely laughed.

The man reached across Camille, money in his fingers. "She is as you described. She will sell quickly."

The man's face was painted in black and white, but the violet-blue eyes sparkled mischievously at her. A glimmer of hope danced in her head but was quickly squelched at the thought that perhaps he truly meant to spirit her away. She shook it off.

Brent tapped her nose with the wad of money. "You know, if you had naught swiped Maggie's diary, this would not be happening to you."

He leaned close, and the aroma of alcohol wafted through her senses. She wrinkled her nose and crunched her face in disgust. He pressed his lips against the filthy rag.

"Adieu, my sweet Camille," he whispered. "Perhaps we shall meet again someday, but do not count on it. I hear Arab princes are very, very possessive."

With those parting words, Brent took his leave, believing himself the smartest young man in New Orleans. As soon as he was out of sight, Reece quickly untied Camille and threw his coat around her shoulders. She snaked her arms about his waist and pulled his warm body close. Burying her head in his chest, she drew on his strength. Her trembling seemed to have increased tenfold, as much from nerves as from the coldness of the tomb.

"He's getting away," she whispered.

"He shan't go far."

She pulled back and looked at him quizzically. He merely smiled. "The constable should be waiting at the entrance by now."

She then noticed that she sat upon a coffin. Brent had taken her to one of the many cemetery vaults in New Orleans. She looked frantically at Reece.

"How did you know where to find me?"

"I didn't," he replied. "After your mother assured me that you were sound asleep, I left and climbed upon your balcony to watch over you. I was afraid Brent would try something. Unfortunately, I fell asleep, and the next thing I knew, someone hit me on the back of my head. When I came to and realized you were gone, I immediately began looking for you. As luck would have it, I ran into a few friends who had seen a figure clad in black with an unconscious girl in his arms running down the streets. So, they helped me find you here."

She placed her hands on both of his cheeks and pulled his

face close to her own. Closing her eyes, she gently kissed him, realizing her heart was lost to this man in black. She pulled back, and he laughed softly. Using his black shirt, he wiped away the black makeup that had smeared all over her mouth and hands. Then he swooped her up and carried her home.

Epilogue

Camille sat in the little room alone. She waited in silence for someone to come for her. She smoothed out the white satin material and fidgeted with the floral bouquet.

The door swung open, and Maggie slipped in. She closed the door quickly behind her, catching her lavender bridesmaid dress in it. A bit embarrassed, she released the fabric from the door before kneeling beside Camille.

"Reece is impatient."

Camille pouted. "I'm sorry. He'll just have to wait. I refuse to marry him without them. It just wouldn't be right."

Maggie dipped her head in acknowledgment. "I am really sorry about what happened. Brent had us all duped. I mean, no one knew the Lafourche's had gambled away all of their fortune."

"Maggie, please, quit apologizing. All is forgiven."

A soft tapping interrupted their intimate conversation. Her mother poked her head in the door. "They're here."

Camille jumped to her feet. "Oh, thank God."

Mrs. du Carte slipped into the room and placed the jewelry box into her daughter's hand. "You know, they really are quite lovely. Perfect heirloom quality."

Biting her lip, Camille opened the box to reveal the ruby earrings she had been accused of stealing. Her thoughts recalled the day Mr. Waldenhorn had arrived on her doorstep with said earrings in hand. He said that just that very day, a gentleman had produced a receipt for them, and the jeweler had apologized profusely.

Camille sighed as the earrings found their rightful place. Then she glanced at the sparkling diamond bracelet on her arm, a gift from Mr. Waldenhorn. Peace filled her as she looked at her MaMa with a warm smile.

"Now I'm ready."

Part 2:

Emily

Chapter 1

February 8, 1890
Saturday, three o'clock in the morning

Emily glared at Brent, who sat across from her in the policeman's coach. Staring fixedly at his hands, he refused to look at her, which only infuriated her more. Before she could stop herself, she kicked him in the shin. That earned her his full attention.

She narrowed her eyes. "Thank you so much, Brent Lafourche. I knew I should not have listened to the likes o' you."

"Careful, sweet, your Irish is leaking out," he whispered, enjoying the opportunity to jab at her pride. He knew she liked to pretend she wasn't Irish. It was a shame her red hair betrayed her more than she was willing to admit.

Emily huffed and tried once more to free herself of the handcuffs. She itched to slap the smug smile off his face. Her mouth dropped as he held his own hands up for her to see. The cuffs dangled loose in his left hand.

"What, how did you—" She thrust her hands out. "Get these off me."

The coach chose that moment to hit a pothole, sending Emily into Brent's lap. Smirking, he wrapped his arms around her and pulled her closer. She squirmed against him but stopped when he seemed to enjoy it. Her green eyes flashed with irritation.

"Let me go," she whispered through clenched teeth.

Without replying, he captured her lips with his. He kissed her until she couldn't breath, enjoying her struggles. When he at last let her go, she gulped in air and quickly pushed away from him.

"Save it for Maggie," she growled. "Wherever she is. I don't suppose God could have caught her as fast as she was running."

Brent shook his head. "Oh, come on, Em. You know Maggie was just a ruse. It's you I want."

"I don't think that's a possibility any more. In light of our current situation, I don't believe we will ever see each other again." The next words unwittingly caught in her throat like bad coffee. "Attempted murder is, after all, a serious offense."

Brent sat back and crossed his arms. "I had no intention of killing Camille, and if you had stayed, you would have found that out."

His cocky manner quickly turned doubtful as he contemplated the upcoming charges. "Although kidnapping and intended slavery might be just as bad."

Both fell into silence as they envisioned what the future held for each of them. Then, Brent moved into action. "I'm not sticking around to find out."

Halfway to the coach door, he looked back at her. "Coming, Em?"

She hesitated, letting the idea of escaping swirl in her head. Something gave her pause, and she shook her head. "No, no I do not believe I am, Brent."

Part of her enjoyed the shocked expression on his face. He was clearly too used to her obliging him in everything he asked. His eyes narrowed suspiciously. "Why not?"

She tilted her head, asking herself that very question. Realizing he was watching her closely, she pulled a mask of indifference over her face and sat back with a bored look. "Because I am tired. Leave me be, Brent." She waved her hands at him as if to shoo him away.

"Fine, suit yourself. I hope you enjoy serving time. Maybe you can ask Camille how she did it." With those parting words, he flung open the door and jumped from the moving coach.

As the carriage pulled to a stop, shouts ensued, and several policemen took off after him. One of them peered in at her, and she looked at him with all the boredom she could muster. "'Twasn't I, sir. Have no fear of that."

A bit chagrined, he nonetheless climbed in and took a seat opposite her. Emily sighed and leaned her head back against the wall of the coach. She closed her eyes, wondering if they would catch Brent. She knew how slick he was. He probably knew the streets of New Orleans better than the policemen.

With one less passenger, the coach moved forward, bringing her closer to her destiny.

* * * *

February 24, 1890
Monday Afternoon

Despite her cavalier attitude, Emily found her hands shaking uncontrollably. She tucked them under her thighs and lifted her chin. She anxiously stared at the judge while he studied the paper in his hand.

Nervously, she looked to her left, making eye contact with her lawyer. On the other side of him sat Maggie, her face so pale she looked ready to faint. For the first time, Emily was truly sorry she had talked her into their shenanigans.

"Emily Ann St. Amande, Margarite Marie Lafitte, please rise."

Closing her eyes, Emily clenched her teeth and forced herself to stand. Her fists belied her inner frustration and fear. Yet she managed to remain calm. She glanced briefly at Maggie and became irritated that she leaned weakly on their lawyer's arm. The least she could do was stand on her own two feet. Refraining from snorting in disgust, Emily thrust out her chin and looked squarely at the judge's face.

"It is the findings of this court that Emily Ann St. Amande and Margarite Marie Lafitte are found guilty of kidnapping. Thus, they are committed to the state for incarceration for a period of twelve months."

The gavel rapped loudly as Maggie broke down in tears. Emily coolly turned her head to the right, meeting the eyes of the prosecuting attorney. She saw neither pleasure nor triumph in Clay du Carte's eyes, merely sadness.

Then she looked behind him to where Camille sat with her new husband. The same look on the father's face was mirrored on the daughter's. Was a chance of forgiveness possible?

Emily quickly turned away, aggravated with herself for thinking such idiotic thoughts. Why should she seek redemption from her? She had no intention of ever coming in contact with Camille again. She would serve her year, and after that, she would be on her way to New York in pursuit of an acting career.

* * * *

March 3, 1890
Monday, seven o'clock in the morning

Emily sat in the parlor, fidgeting nervously with the simple green traveling dress. She nearly jumped out of her skin when the knock came at the front door. As their servant answered it, she stood in the parlor doorway, twisting a strand of red hair between her fingers.

Ms. Ridgemont's plump form filled the foyer. "Is my charge ready?"

The butler stepped aside, allowing the woman further inside. She looked around, first spotting the five suitcases. She shook her head.

"You are only allowed two cases," she clucked.

Mr. St. Amande appeared and introductions were made. "Allow me to introduce your charge. My daughter, Emily."

Cold, assessing eyes turned on the girl, and she squirmed. Several long seconds later, Ms. Ridgemont asked, "Might I have a word with your daughter in private, Mr. St. Amande?"

"Certainly," he said, a bit startled at the request.

Emily backed into the parlor as Ms. Ridgemont descended upon her like a bull. The matron closed the door and turned to her with hands on hips.

"I believe an explanation is in order."

Emily looked at her queerly. "For what?"

"Your attire."

Emily glanced down at her dress. "I see nothing the matter with my attire. In fact, 'tis quite the fashion."

"The standard uniform of a Louisiana convict is gray, and that dress, my dear, is not gray. I must insist you change immediately."

Emily's eyes narrowed, and she pursed her lips. "No."

The matron looked incredulously at her. "I am afraid you must not have heard me correctly. I said: you must change."

Emily's nose rose up. "Make me."

Ms. Ridgemont's jaw dropped briefly before her face darkened with fury. In a flash, her hand reached out, grasped the front of the dress and pulled with all she dared. Fabric ripped, buttons popped, and Emily cried out in horror.

Smiling smugly, the matron turned on her heel. "I'll check with your mother to see which case holds the required attire."

Glaring at the woman's back, Emily growled through clenched teeth. "My mother's dead, you cussed old bat."

The woman whirled around, shocked at the obscenities pouring forth from the young lady's mouth. "You had best watch your tongue, missy. I do not know what kind of gutter trash you have been associating with, but that kind of talk will not be tolerated."

"Really? And just what do you think you shall do about it?" Emily challenged, trying to appear tough and hold up the bodice of her dress at the same time.

Ms. Ridgemont pulled herself up as straight as possible and backed Emily into a corner. "For starters, every curse word slipping from your mouth will ensure a slap from the back of my hand."

Emily sneered, not truly believing. "Yeah, right." She hesitated but the urge was just too compelling. "Dang old crab."

Shock settled on her face as a stinging slap smarted her left cheek. It was hard enough to hurt yet not enough to bruise. Her mouth dropped, and her free hand balled up into a fist. Realizing she was only making it worse, she closed her eyes and counted to ten.

Wisely, Ms. Ridgemont backed away, allowing the chit to gain control of her emotions. As nonchalantly as possible, she made her way toward the door. "I shall find your gray dresses," she paused and looked back over her shoulder. "You do have gray dresses, do you not?"

Reluctantly, Emily nodded. "They are in the matching gray trunk," she whispered.

"Good. I shall fetch you one. Wait here."

"I would not dream of doing any thing else."

Fifteen minutes later, the two women were settled into the coach and headed to the train station.

Chapter 2

"You mean to tell me that you do not have a chaperone? Oh no," Ms. Ridgemont huffed. "This will not do. No, 'twill not do at all."

The sun pounded down on Emily's head as she stood a few steps behind Ms. Ridgemont. As the back porch was cast in shadows, she could not see the man standing there. Even shading her eyes lent not a bit of help in that direction. She shifted from foot to foot.

"I'm sorry, ma'am. I've been so busy what with running the farm that I've had no time to get one. Why, I wouldn't even know where to look at the moment, seeing as how this is the only female convict I've ever hired to work here."

The word *farm* stuck in Emily's ears. She looked around, seeing her surroundings for the first time. She had been told she was going to a plantation, not a farm. Yet, the fields were vast and filled with workers, and the house itself was huge. *Why,* she thought, *it even has a name.*

"Sir, I believe the correct term is *plantation* not *farm*," she chimed in. "Hence the name, Cypress Plantation."

All eyes focused on her. "Ma'am, round here, we prefer farm. It's easier on the tongue."

Emily rolled her eyes. "Suit yourself, and it is *miss,* not *ma'am.* I am eighteen, not thirty."

The matronly woman shot an irritated glance at her charge then looked back at the man. "I see no other recourse then. I shall stay until an adequate chaperone has been acquired."

A small groan escaped Emily. The only thing that had made the trip bearable was the thought that she would soon be free of Mrs. Ogre. Now she would have to suffer the overbearing she-devil until who knew when. Grumpily, she followed the woman into the house.

"Mr. McCabe, if you would show us to our quarters, I believe we should like to freshen up." Ms. Ridgemont wiped the sweat off her brow, gasping for breath. Though it was only the beginning of March, the humidity was stifling.

He stopped several feet ahead and turned around. One hand rested on his hip while the other scratched the back of his head. His ruggedly handsome face was filled with awkwardness.

"Well," he drawled. "Seems we have a bit of a problem in that respect. I wasn't prepared for two of ya."

Ms. Ridgemont raised a weary eyebrow at him. "Where were you planning on Miss Emily sleeping, sir?"

A brief moment of silence had Emily's heart racing. *To be sure he's handsome. But surely he does not think—*

"In the baby's room, ma'am."

Both guardian and charge let out held breaths. The tension drained out of their faces, and Emily felt a huge measure of relief.

"Seeing as how she's here to take care of little Jacob, I thought it best if she stayed in his room," he said innocently.

Emily's eyes widened. "I am not a baby sitter, sir. House chores," she stumbled on the words. "I am here to help with the cleaning and such, am I not?"

Once again, Ms. Ridgemont shot a warning look at her

before smiling sweetly at Mr. McCabe. "Why, surely a house this big must have empty rooms, sir."

"Yes, ma'am. Completely empty. We're not accustomed to having any company."

"Oh, I see. Well then, we will simply share the room."

He grimaced. "Well, the bed is a single."

Not missing a beat, the matron stated, "'Twill not be a problem. My charge is young. She can sleep on the floor."

Emily's shoulders sagged, and her jaw dropped. *As if things are not bad enough.*

A tiny Indian woman chose that moment to enter the kitchen. She carried a small bundle in her arms. She looked Emily up and down disapprovingly.

"Lucas, how she gonna be a fit wet nurse? She got no breasts. Where she get milk to feed this baby?"

"I've explained that to you, Rayna," he replied. His face reddened with embarrassment. "We have cow's milk. She's just here to take care of him."

"Hmpf."

"Ms. Ridgemont, Miss Emily, this is my cook, Rayna. She's of the Cherokee tribe and been with me since I was a baby."

While Ms. Ridgemont made pleasantries, Emily stared coldly at the squaw. She started to cross her arms, but the handcuffs stopped her. Awkwardly, she let her hands drop in front of her.

"I believe she'll have a hard time holding little Jacob with those on," Mr. McCabe pointed out.

At Ms. Ridgemont's indication, the two constables with them took the cuffs off. She rubbed her tender wrists. She had been forced to wear them the entire trip. She smiled ruefully, thinking, *Why, 'tis as if Ms. Ridgemont does not trust me.*

Watching her charge's face, Ms. Ridgemont whispered,

"Do not think to run, lass, they shan't be far away if need be." She patted the pocket where she had put the handcuffs. At Mr. McCabe's curious expression, she stated, "The girl can be a handful, sir, but don't you worry. I know how to handle her kind."

Before Emily had a chance to explode, Rayna placed the baby in her arms. "Here, I need a cigarette."

Emily's mouth watered. "Ooo, I'd love a Duke." She thought of the Duke of Durham cigarettes in her closet at home.

"Young ladies do not smoke," Ms. Ridgemont stated haughtily.

"But—"

She held her hand up to prevent further discussion. Turning on her heel, she addressed the plantation owner. "Our room, Mr. McCabe?"

* * * *

Emily sat in a rocking chair by the window. It was so hot that Ms. Ridgemont had allowed her to strip down to her chemise. She closed her eyes, reveling in the breeze dancing across her skin. The baby lay sleeping in her arms, for which she was grateful. The two had made a horrible acquaintance. The infant had decided to wail at the top of his lungs until Rayna had brought up some milk.

Now, she held the empty nursing bottle loosely in her right hand. She feared to move lest the baby wake and start that awful racket again. *No. Better to stay put as it seems to work for the moment.*

The only thing breaking the silence was the loud snoring coming from the she-devil. The old bag had rinsed with water and climbed into bed for her afternoon nap.

This would have been a perfect opportunity for an escape attempt. The door had no locks, and the constables had left to return to New Orleans. The only problem was the baby. She was afraid that if she put the baby in his crib, he'd wake up screaming.

Sighing, Emily studied Jacob as he slept. His thick, dark eyelashes rested on sweet chubby cheeks. He smiled, cooing softly with content.

"You and I have much in common, Jake," she whispered. "My mother's gone as well. Though mine at least waited thirteen years."

The thread of a common bond linked her heart to the babe. She frowned at the thought that his mother had never even held him. From what she had been told, the delivery had been especially hard, and the poor woman had died during childbirth.

Get a grip, Em, she thought, shaking herself.

Making her resolve, she grasped the baby close and slowly got to her feet. She cringed as the rocking chair creaked loudly. She stopped it with her toe, making sure the Ogre-lady stayed asleep. Then, as carefully as possible, she laid Jacob face down in his crib.

Covering him with a blanket, she rubbed his back softly. Then, she quickly donned her gray dress and tiptoed to the door. She looked back over her shoulder, ensuring the Ogress still slept. Satisfied, she quietly opened the door and slipped out of the room.

Amazingly, she made it out of the plantation and all the way out to the stables without seeing a single soul. She paused before one of the horses. Her hand ran down its brown velvet nose.

She couldn't get Jake out of her mind. If she stayed, she could make a difference in his life. If she left, heaven only knew what would happen to the babe, not to mention the fact that there would be hell to pay if she were caught.

I must be insane, she thought. *Just go. Who cares about some brat that isn't even mine?'*

Absentmindedly, her fingers touched her flat stomach. *But it could have been.*

"Beautiful mare, isn't she? Although, if you're planning on escaping, you might want to choose the other one. The one you picked is quite spirited."

Chapter 3

Emily jumped and turned around. Quickly composing herself, she raised her nose and crossed her arms. "You startled me."

On the other side of the barn, Lucas McCabe leaned casually against a stall, chewing on a piece of sugar cane. He regarded her with a sense of boredom, fully indicating that he had calculated her intentions a long time before she had thought of them herself.

"I had hoped that as a lady of breeding, we would not have to resort to locks and cuffs," he said.

A rush of warmth heated Emily's cheeks. "I...I was just getting some fresh air," she stammered. "I was not—"

He held up his hand. "Please, save yourself the trouble." He then pointed at her. "I'll give you one more chance."

Emily swallowed nervously and nodded. She forced the words out of her mouth. "Thank you, Mr. McCabe."

He pushed away from the wall. "Now, I believe your duties await you in the nursery."

"Mr. McCabe, I fear there has been a tragic mistake. You see," Emily paused, unsure of how to proceed. "I know nothing about babies."

His brows furrowed with confusion. "But the warden said you had a seven month old baby brother."

It was Emily's turn to be confused. "Did he? Why on earth..."

Then it dawned on her, and her face lightened in understanding. "Oh, he must have mistaken me for Maggie. She's the one with a baby brother, not I."

It was clear the mix up didn't phase Lucas one bit. He simply shrugged. "Well, I am sure as a woman it'll come naturally to you. Besides, Rayna will teach you what you need to know."

Irritation sparked in Emily's eyes. "What a chauvinistic thing to say."

"Excuse me?"

Emily's embarrassment at being caught quickly turned into anger. "The fact that I am a female does not mean that I know a damn thing about taking care of a baby." Her hands rested on her hips as her eyes flickered dangerously. "I suppose therefore that I am a shoo in for baking apple pies, darning your socks and playing the pianoforte."

Luke's eyes widened in surprise. "Well," he drawled, "Seems I stepped on a rattler."

Flabbergasted at being referred to as a snake, Emily opened and closed her mouth twice before sticking her nose in the air. "Hmpf."

As lady-like as possible, she sashayed past him and out of the barn. She felt his eyes laughing at her as he followed her to the house, but she refused to give a damn. Her demeanor changed instantly at the sight of Ms. Ridgemont on the back porch.

"Tried to escape, I see."

Before Emily had a chance to reply, Luke spoke. "I was just showing her my new mare, Ms. Ridgemont. It's my fault for not telling you."

Shocked, Emily looked at Luke. He merely raised a conspiratorial eyebrow at her and smiled charmingly. "It seems she needed some exercise after the long journey, and I thought a trip to the barn might prove interesting."

Emily watched the disappointment play across Ms. Ridgemont's face and felt a tad sorry for her. "Oh, come now, Ms. Ridgemont, I'm sure I'll do something soon that you may reprimand me for," she smiled sweetly. "For now, though, I was hoping we could enjoy some lemonade."

"I know I sure could use some," Luke said.

As he walked up the steps, Emily found herself admiring the way he filled out his jeans. A smile touched her lips. *Dear me, but he has a lovely——*

"Ladies?"

Coming to her senses, she saw he held the door for them. Her cheeks reddened at where her thoughts had gone, and she ducked her head as she entered the house, unable to make eye contact with him. The second she stepped inside, the baby began to wail.

* * * *

Emily stared down at the crying baby, unsure of what to do. She couldn't fathom he was hungry again. Awkwardly, she picked him up, almost dropping him when the cloth diaper squished against her hand. She made a face as a certain smell reached her nose.

"Ugh, how disgusting," she exclaimed, quickly setting him back in his crib. He began to cry harder. "I see you don't care that much for it either, do you, Jake?"

Even though she had never changed a diaper in her life, she realized she had to learn fast. She unhooked the pins and pulled back the cloth, pursing her lips and holding her breath at the same time. As a stream of urine hit her square in the face, she screamed in disgust and backed away from the crib.

Seconds later, Rayna and Luke appeared in the doorway.

Emily looked at them with horror. "He...he urinated on me."

The fact that they both had to suppress smiles infuriated Emily. She stomped her foot. "'Tis not funny."

Moving into action, Rayna swept past her. "Best clean up, Miss Emily. I'll finish changing Jacob."

Luke flashed her a smile before slipping back down stairs. She growled softly, wishing she had something to throw at him.

* * * *

"Osda unelanvhi!" Rayna exclaimed a day later as she entered the nursery. The stench was unbearable.

Emily looked up from her position by the open window. She had been watching the workers in the sugar cane field. "Pardon me?"

"It means good God." The squaw wrinkled her nose and looked around for the source. Her gaze paused on the diaper hamper. "You not clean diapers," she fussed. "Baby need clean cloth and nice smelling room."

It suddenly dawned on Emily where the awful smell was coming from. "You expect me to clean those?"

Rayna crossed her arms. "Asehi."

Emily wrinkled her mouth in confusion. "What?"

Frustrated, Rayna almost yelled at her. "Yes."

Jacob woke at the loud sound and immediately began crying. Emily's shoulders sagged in defeat. "Now look at what you've done. It took me forever to get him down."

Rayna grabbed hold of Jacob before Emily could. "Oh, no. I watch him while you clean cloth. Missy not get off that easy."

Emily glared at the squaw. Through clenched teeth, she asked, "Where do I clean them?"

* * * *

From her position on the back porch, Emily gleefully

watched as Ms. Ridgemont stood uncertainly by the waiting carriage. A message had arrived that morning stating that her father had been involved in a serious carriage accident. Thus, the matron had no choice but to leave.

"I have yet to be convinced that Rayna will be an appropriate chaperone," Ms. Ridgemont clucked. Shaking her head, she reluctantly allowed Luke to assist her into the carriage.

"I promise there's no need to worry, ma'am," Luke assured. "Why, she may be tiny, but she's gotta will of thunder."

"Hmpf," she replied, settling back into her seat. "And I promise you, Mr. McCabe, as soon as I get a chance, I shall provide you with a chaperone. An Indian squaw—"

"Thank you, Ms. Ridgemont. Have a safe trip."

With those parting words, he closed the door in her face and indicated the driver to be on his way. When he turned to Emily, she saw anger in his eyes.

"What an insufferable—" he paused, struggling for a polite curse word.

"Cantankerous old crab?" Emily offered.

Surprised, he looked at her. Then a slow smile spread across his face. "Exactly."

Chapter 4

April 1, 1890
Tuesday

Emily sat on the porch steps with Jacob. She held his tiny hands firmly as she balanced him on her knees. His giggles filled the air as she bounced her legs, and she couldn't help but laugh with him. Over the weeks, the two had formed a bond.

Something made her look up, and the sight of Luke approaching made her heart jump. Then she noticed the urgency of his pace, and as he drew near, she wondered why he frowned.

He stopped at her feet, seemingly surprised to find himself there. Without a word, he sat beside her, placing his elbows on his knees. He stared despondently at the ground.

"What's wrong, Mr. McCabe?"

He sighed wearily. "One of the convicts lost his foot today."

"Oh my," Emily breathed.

"A water moccasin bit him, but the foreman didn't tell anyone until it was too late," Luke growled. He ran a callused hand through dark hair, then hung his head. "Damn it all."

"Why didn't he tell?"

Luke raised his head and looked at her. "Because he's a mean son of a..." He stopped himself. While he knew she wasn't adverse to it, he was reluctant to curse in front of her. "Well, he'll have to take his aggression out some place else. I fired him."

Then he jumped to his feet and walked out a few steps. He turned to her with his left hand on his hip and gestured wildly with his right as he talked. "I try to instill a positive atmosphere here. It seems to work much better than brutality, but when you're sabotaged..."

Rayna spoke from her position on the porch swing. "You best watch your back then, Lucas. That man never like you, and he lose face when you fire him."

His frown deepened, and he sat back down with his head in his hands. Jacob chose that moment to pull a handful of his father's hair.

"Da-da."

Luke's head snapped up. "Did he just say—"

Emily nodded, smiling widely. "Yes." She kissed the baby on the cheek. "Perfect timing, Jake."

Luke took hold of his son, easing his mind for the next ten minutes while he played with the boy. As soon as the baby became cranky, though, he quickly handed him back to Emily.

"Well, I need to wash up before dinner," he stated. He hesitated, watching Jake cuddle close to Emily. "I think on Saturday, we'll let the workers rest. I'll send a handful in the morning to catch some crawfish, and they can boil 'em."

Emily's eyes lit up. "Ooo, I love crawfish."

Luke raised an eyebrow. "What would a lady such as yourself know about a poor man's food?"

She raised her nose. "Hmpf, they sell crawfish in the Quarter."

"Well, don't get any ideas. You're not going."

"What?"

"It's not for the likes of you."

"Excuse me?" Her temper rose.

"I believe Ms. Ridgemont would agree that mingling with a bunch of male convicts would not be in your best interest."

The corners of her mouth drooped, and her spirits sunk. "Oh, I see." She fought back the unexpected tears. Clutching Jacob close, she rose to her feet.

"I believe Jake needs changing," she whispered, hoping the coldness of her tone hid the hurt. She rushed inside, missing the befuddled look that crossed Luke's face.

* * * *

April 5, 1890
Saturday, Late Morning

"I really think that Miss Emily should accompany us," Luke protested.

His mother-in-law practically snatched Jake out of Emily's arms. The woman refused to look her in the eye and immediately presented her with a view of her back. When the boy whimpered, his grandmama patted his back in an attempt to sooth, but his tears only increased.

"Nonsense," she replied. "I am quite capable of taking care of him on our little Saturday picnic. Let the girl have the day off. Even convicts deserve a break every now and again."

Crossing her arms, Emily glared at the back of the woman's coiffed head. Her hands itched to yank at the blonde hair. Then her gaze shifted to Luke, noticing his discomfort as he stood beside his father-in-law.

It dawned on her how amusing the situation had become, and she allowed herself a rueful smile. The arrival of his prior in-laws last night had caught him off guard. The completely-in-control plantation owner had become the not-quite-good-enough son-in-law.

Why, she thought, *I bet he believes they think he is the cause of their precious daughter's death.*

Emily blinked, breaking the spell her thoughts had woven around her. "Mr. McCabe," she smiled weakly, placing a weary look on her face. "I do feel a tad unwell. Perhaps it would be best."

He locked eyes with her, clearly seeing through her ruse, but as he opened his mouth to speak, so did Mrs. Shreve.

"Heaven forbid she should pass a cold onto Jacob." She snapped her fingers. "Henry, Lucas, I'm ready to go."

Her husband opened the front door for her, and she swept by with Jacob bawling. The sight touched Emily's heart, and she frowned, fighting the desire to rip the boy out of the old viper's arms.

Luke took a step toward her, intent on chastising her for assisting in his entrapment, but his father-in-law unwittingly intervened.

"Are you coming, Lucas?" Mr. Shreve asked as he followed his wife.

Luke glanced from Emily to the door and then back at her. With a frustrated, low growl, he took off after his in-laws. Emily let go of the breath she'd been holding, but jumped as the door slammed shut in Luke's angry wake.

* * * *

A half hour later, Emily slipped on a pair of Luke's trouser pants. She cinched the extra fabric around her tiny waist with one of his belts, but had no idea what to do with the cloth that covered her feet completely. At first, she thought of rolling the pant leg, but she noticed a dusty pair of work boots in the closet. She discovered that the size of his foot was just a size or two bigger than hers. She would just have to walk slowly.

Then she pinned up her hair and covered it with a huge straw hat. Looking in the mirror, she dipped her head, hoping she could pass for a man. Luke's old work clothes made her look shabby enough, and along with her five foot, seven inch stature and thin frame, she judged she could pass for a young man. 'Tis what she hoped, anyway.

Try to keep me from having fun, she thought, smirking as she headed out of the house. *I'll show him.*

"Well," drawled the man on the porch swing. "It's about time."

* * * *

Despite the fact that she kept tripping in the borrowed boots, Emily managed to keep pace with Luke. She had been somewhat amazed to find him in such a jovial mood, regardless of the fact that she had been caught red-handed. While she should have been happy to have gotten her way, she couldn't help feeling chagrined.

They soon stepped onto the path which led to the area that had once held slaves but now held convicts. The sudden sound of male voices and laughter made Emily pause. Her courage failed. Her pulse caught in her throat, and she thought herself mad for attempting to go there alone among obvious ruffians.

When Luke realized she held back, he shook his head, retraced his steps and grabbed her wrist. "Uh-uh. No stopping now, Miss Emily." He pulled her forward unmercifully. "Your crawfish await you."

Emily gulped and thrust up her chin. She gritted her teeth in determination as Luke led them between houses, past guards and into an open area. The number of gray and black striped outfits staggered her, and she unwittingly held tighter to Luke's hand. As he found a spot for them at one of the tables, she realized she would have made a seriously grave error if she had attempted this alone.

When he at last let go of her, she wished he hadn't. She pressed closer to him, feeling unsafe without the feel of his hand in hers. All eyes seemed to focus on them, and she stared at the boiled crawfish before her. Luke's voice rumbled loudly as he bade them to continue.

He gave her a nudge. "Eat."

Feeling weak, she obediently picked up a crawfish and broke off the tail, discarding the head. The man next to her noticed and smirked. "What, you don't suck the head?"

She blanched. "No," she whispered, not daring to look at him. Then, she gulped and put forth a more forceful no.

The men resumed their conversations, and as she solemnly partook of the meal, she tried unsuccessfully to tune out their colorful language. She had only thought she had heard vulgarity in the French Quarter. These men took it to a new level.

A short time later, Luke leaned down and whispered in her ear, "Have you had enough?"

Certain her cheeks flamed red, her pride overrode her embarrassment. "These are so delicious. I cannot seem to get full."

"Okay," he drawled, amused at her discomfort.

Only after creating three large piles of empty crawfish shells did Emily declare that she was finished. She gulped down the fourth glass of lemonade and then carefully dabbed at her mouth with the hem of her shirt. She fought down an unladylike burp, but in the end managed to cover her mouth just in time with the back of her hand.

Sheepishly, she snuck a peek to see if Luke had heard. He merely watched her antics with a bemused grin. "As the German's say, Miss Emily, it's not bad manners, just good food."

After swigging down his own drink, he took her hand. "I suggest we return to the house. If Ms. Ridgemont knew I allowed you down here, she'd have my hide. Besides—"

The sound of fighting stopped him, and he looked around. Finding the source, they watched as the guards quickly broke it up. Then, dragging her along with him, he approached the rabble-rousers. One was held by a guard. The other lay on the ground holding his arm. Blood gushed from a long, deep gash.

Emily gasped, not from the sight of blood but from recognition. The man with the knife wound was no other than Brent Lafourche.

Chapter 5

April 8, 1890
Tuesday, Mid-Morning

Emily lay on the nursery room floor, watching Jake play with his toys. Her mind drifted to the other day when she'd first seen Brent. Their eyes had locked briefly before Luke stepped in front of her and blocked her view. Shortly thereafter, he had escorted her back to the house. She was grateful that she and Brent had not talked.

Isn't it just like fickle fate to bring us together again? Emily wondered sleepily. *Of all the plantations, he had to end up here. He better not screw this up for me. For a change, things seem to be going well.*

Emily's eyes drooped until she couldn't keep them open. The next thing she knew, something hit her on the head. Startled awake, she looked into Jake's innocent little face in front of her. He then hit her on the head with another toy and watched for her reaction. After exclaiming in pain, she growled, "Jake, what did you do that for?"

Emily struggled to control her temper. "That was a very bad thing to do, Jake. Very bad."

She sat up, rubbing her temple. Then she cast an aggravated look at the boy. His expression soon turned from a frown to full-fledged crying. She sighed and quickly picked him up. "Golly, Jake, it's okay. Don't cry."

Walking back and forth, she patted his back. "If you would just not wake up in the middle of the night and let me get some sleep, I think we'd all be happier. Maybe then I wouldn't feel so grouchy all the time."

She sat down in the rocking chair, hushing him in an effort to sooth him. His tears soon died down to whimpers, and then she finally found him asleep in her arms. She shook her head and continued to rock. With her arms wrapped tightly around him, she quickly fell asleep, too.

* * * *

Emily woke the instant the child was lifted from her sleeping arms. Rayna smiled fondly at her. "Young Jake become night owl, eh?"

Emily smiled sleepily and nodded. She stretched, raising her arms high in the air. Luke chose that moment to enter the room. She dropped her arms immediately, feeling awkward as he simply stared at her with a strange look on his face. A blush rose in her cheeks as she could only imagine what he had been thinking at seeing her bosom thrust out.

He cleared his throat awkwardly and put his hands in his pockets. Shuffling his feet, he chose to hover over the crib as Rayna put the sleeping infant down.

"Would you like to see the new colt?" he asked, seemingly to no one in particular.

Startled, Emily stared at his back. She was unsure if he was talking to her or to Rayna. Then she looked at the squaw, who smiled as if she knew a secret.

"You go, Miss Emily, I listen for Jake."

* * * *

Emily leaned against the white fence. The small colt pressed close to his mother, too scared of the bigger horses in the field to stray. He was deep velvet brown. The color of Luke's eyes, she noted. There wasn't a speck of white anywhere on the colt. It was a wonder, as his father was completely white.

"Do you ride?" Luke asked. He stood close to her, and it seemed every nerve in her body could sense he was there.

"No. I've never had the opportunity, but I've loved horses since I was little," she replied. "I think my mother and father were scared that I might get hurt."

"Well, that's always a possibility."

As a heavy silence descended upon them, Emily could not resist the pull of his stare. Though she blushed profusely, she met his eyes boldly and became lost in the warmth of brown fire. He placed his hand under her chin, and before she could comprehend his intentions, his lips were pressed to hers in a soft kiss.

Almost instantly, he pulled back. "I'm sorry," he whispered huskily. "I shouldn't have done that."

Forcing herself not to step toward him, she softly said, "Would I be too bold if I said I didn't mind?"

In answer, he closed the small space separating them and pulled her into a more passionate embrace. This time, his tongue slipped past her lips, filling her mouth like warm velvet coffee. Closing her eyes, she sank into his spell, luxuriating in the comfortableness of his arms. Emily couldn't shake the feeling that she had at last come home; that she was right where she was supposed to be.

A few minutes later, they parted, and a sudden awkwardness claimed them both as they remembered who and where they were. Luke took a few more steps back, placed his hand on his hip and ran the other through his hair in consternation.

"I shouldn't have done that," he stated again, refusing to

meet her eyes.

Misinterpreting his reaction, Emily threw her defenses up. "No, I guess you shouldn't have. I daresay, I am not that easily led into a man's bed," she exclaimed and turned her back on him. She crossed her arms and started to head back toward the house. She touched her lips, however, in remembrance of that devastating kiss.

A hand grabbed her shoulder from behind and caused her to turn around. The warmth in his eyes sent the butterflies in her stomach straight to her heart, but something else flickered in the brown depths and gave her pause.

"That's not what I meant." He hesitated, struggling to find the right words. "I'm your guardian. I should know better than to take advantage of you."

"No man takes advantage of me unless I want him to," she stated haughtily.

Placing both hands on his hips, Luke looked at the ground, shook his head and sighed heavily. "I ain't gonna deny that I'm attracted to you, Miss Emily, but you're eighteen. I'm twenty-three, and you're under my care. It ain't gonna work out."

Emily's eyes narrowed, and she pursed her lips. "Because I'm a convict."

The corners of his mouth turned down. "I don't give a damn 'bout that."

"Then what is it, Mr. McCabe?" she demanded. Her heart fluttered wildly. "Did you think that I would hand out favors simply because I'm a convict?"

Confusion crossed his face as he contemplated just what he had done. "You're right. It was damn foolish of me," he growled. "I got chores ta do. I suggest you go see to Jake."

He turned on his heel, leaving her to gape at him. When he rounded the corner of the barn, her astonishment turned to anger as she realized he wasn't going to give her a straight answer.

"That son of a bitch," she whispered and started after him, intent on giving him a piece of her mind.

* * * *

Mrs. Shreve stepped out of the barn and watched the little convict race after her son-in-law. She slapped her riding crop against her thigh, heedless of its sting. A white ring formed around a mouth that was screwed up tight with aggravation.

How dare that little trollop, she thought, grateful she had followed her instincts and ridden over to see her grandson.

She retraced her steps back to her mare. She knew exactly what had to be done, and there wasn't a second to lose.

* * * *

Emily stopped walking when she realized that she had lost sight of her prey. Hands on hips, she huffed as she looked up and down the dirt road, trying to determine where he had gone. Then she spied the small path that led into the woods and quickly followed it.

She stopped when she reached the edge of the woods. All her anger died at the sight of him kneeling at a grave in the middle of a fenced in cemetery. She stepped back into the shadows as it became clear. He was, and probably always would be, in love with his dead wife.

As her heart burned in her chest, she bit back a sob and rushed back down the path. She knew she had no right to ever expect his love, but the knowledge hurt nonetheless.

Chapter 6

April 14, 1890
Monday

"Luke, I'd like to introduce Mrs. Rachel Dominique, your new chaperone for the convict watching Jake."

Emily looked up from her position on the floor to the hallway where Luke stood at the front door. Her cheeks became hot at being referred to as a convict. She got to her feet and self-consciously dusted off the skirt of her gray dress. Jake continued playing, heedless of anything but his toys.

Luke glanced in her direction briefly before stepping aside to let the newcomers in. He had barely spoken to her since that day by the barn, and she had not tried to draw him into conversation. She did remember the telephone ringing that very evening, and as it rarely rang, the sound had been disturbingly loud. She had wondered at the time who it was, and now she had a pretty good idea.

Damn him she thought. *It's not like I kissed him. He opened the can of worms, not I.*

A petite young woman of about twenty stepped almost regally into the foyer. The black satin of her gown quietly swished as she walked. She daintily held out her gloved hand for Luke, and Emily almost laughed as he shook it like it was another man's. It was obvious he had not been raised in high society, and she wondered how he'd won the heart of Jake's mother.

"Nice to meet you, Mrs. Dominique."

"Please, call me Rachel."

Luke then introduced Emily, and although Rachel was polite, her attention quickly returned to Luke.

"Rachel's husband died about a year ago," informed Mrs. Shreve. She lowered her voice. "Killed in a gun fight while on so-called business in Texas. His insurance policy refused to pay and poor Rachel is, well, destitute."

The little blonde's cheeks appropriately flamed red, and she looked at the ground in dismay. "I don't know what I would do without Mrs. Shreve's kindness."

Luke raised a wary eyebrow but managed to keep his opinions to himself. "Well, let's get your belongings and get you settled in. I'm sure my mother-in-law is anxious to get back home."

The older lady turned towards Jake. "Oh, not just yet. There's plenty of time for me to get back to the heart of Baton Rouge. I want to spend the afternoon with my grandson."

A thought suddenly occurred to Emily, and she blurted it out before she could stop herself. "I'm not sleeping on the floor again."

All eyes turned to her, and she crossed her arms defensively and refused to look away from Luke. She noted with satisfaction that his own face turned a shade redder, but his eyes darkened dangerously. "No, Emily, you won't. I've had a bed set up in the room across from your's and Jake's."

Emily furrowed her eyebrows as she tried to recall when he could have done it without her knowing. "When did you do that?"

"The day you and Jake went to town with Rayna."

"Oh." A bit deflated, Emily refused to back down. "So you did it while my back was turned."

Rachel touched Luke's arm, breaking the tension in the room and effectively changing the topic of conversation. "My trunks are outside."

Before following Rachel out of the house, Luke shot a warning glance at Emily. She bristled, but as she went to focus her attention on Jake, she saw that Mrs. Shreve had beaten her to it. Not knowing what to do, she took a seat by the window and quietly sulked.

* * * *

As there was a guest in the house, it fell upon Luke to assume his duties as host. Thus, it was necessary for a formal dinner. Rayna saw to the preparation of the meal and asked Emily to set the table.

As she lingered in the formal dinning room, her thoughts took wing, and she pictured herself seated next to Luke instead of Rachel. In actuality, of course, there was not a place set for her, as she was considered a servant. Her spirits felt heavy, but she consoled herself.

I don't really want to be in the same room with him anyway.

Her fingers lingered on the fine silver, thinking of home. The nightly formality of dinner had ceased upon her mother's death. Her father had buried himself in work, and so she had taken to eating alone. It had been dreadfully lonely, but one could put down one's guard. No one was there to care whether she ate with the salad fork or with her fingers. She supposed Rachel's table etiquette was of the utmost perfection.

She sneered at the thought. She dreaded the time she would have to spend with her so-called chaperone. In truth, the lady should have stayed locked up in her own home for the entirety of the customary mourning period. She must be in sore need indeed to have breeched such etiquette.

Then she thought about the quiet dinners she had shared in the kitchen with Luke, Rayna and Jake, but that was before the kiss. After that, he had avoided her as much as possible, which meant working late in the fields.

She sighed and turned to go help Rayna in the kitchen, only to stop dead still at the sight of Luke all dressed up. He stared at her with a mixture of desire and what looked like guilt. She resisted the urge to gawk at him like a moon-struck schoolgirl. Although, she did take a sideways peek as she darted past him. So intent on escaping his presence, she ran right into Rachel.

"Oh," exclaimed the widow. "Pardon me."

"No," Emily cooed with just a hint of sarcasm. "'Twas my fault. I do so apologize."

Quickly composing herself, the blonde stated airily, "'Tis not a problem, dear."

She sashayed into the dining room, and Emily hesitated a few steps out of sight but not out of sound. Her eyes narrowed as Rachel fawned over Luke.

"I made this mourning garter for you this afternoon," Rachel's words dripped with honey. "I am surprised Mrs. Shreve overlooked this when your wife died."

"Well," Luke drawled. "To be quite honest, she didn't. I've just been busy running the plantation and all. Besides, I hardly have company."

"Until now."

Crossing her arms, Emily rolled her eyes. Rayna suddenly appeared with a platter of food, and Emily jumped to attention. The squaw scowled and muttered, "She servant, too. Why we put on airs for her?"

Emily shrugged innocently. "Please don't ask me to serve them," she begged.

Rayna nodded in understanding. "Go feed Jake. I can handle this."

Gratefully, Emily escaped into the kitchen, only to have her heart lodge in her throat at the sight of Brent eating at the table.

"What the hell are you doing?" Emily whispered angrily.

Brent innocently looked up from his meal. "Why, eating, of course."

She crossed her arms in frustration and tapped her foot. "Field convicts don't eat in the house."

"They do when they've been reassigned," he grinned slyly.

Her mouth started to open, but she caught herself in time. *First Miss Etiquette,* she thought angrily, *Now Mr. Troublemaker.*

Brent watched her with amusement. "Ah, there's that Irish fired I missed so much."

She narrowed her eyes. "How?"

Brent raised his right arm. It was bandaged from fingers to elbow. "I'm not of much use in the fields, and there are already plenty of cooks. I convinced the guards I'd do an excellent job doing the manly chores up here. They spoke to Mr. McCabe, and voila, here I am."

Emily smelled a rat. "I don't know what game you're playing, Brent, but leave me out of it. Things are going well for me, and you're not going to mess it up."

Rayna entered the kitchen, and Emily turned to her in frustration. She pointed at Brent. "He shouldn't be here."

"Mr. McCabe said he work for me now," the squaw stated. "'Bout time, too. House need lots of repairs I can't do."

"But," Emily protested, unsure of how to state her case. "He...he'll escape."

Amused, Brent pushed away from the table and showed her his shackled feet. "How far will I get with these on?"

"Oh, like that will stop you," she sneered.

Brent managed a shocked expression. "Miss Emily," he chided.

Rayna looked quizzically at her. "But, Mr. McCabe say that he say you vouch for him."

"What?" Emily yelled.

Rayna continued. "And based on your good behavior, he allow the fellow up here."

"Of all the ridiculous... He didn't even ask me if I knew him," Emily exploded.

"Do you?"

Emily turned to find Luke leaning against the doorframe. The sight of him chased all her thoughts hither and yon. She gulped, trying to decide how to proceed.

"Well? I have a guest waiting for me, Miss Emily. I'd like an answer," Luke demanded.

Through clenched teeth, she replied, "Yes, I know him."

"Good. Then it's settled." He started to return to the dining room.

"But just because I know him doesn't mean I vouch for him."

Luke stopped and looked back at her. "So what are you saying, Miss Emily?"

The sound of a baby's rattle drew her eye to Brent. Seemingly innocent, he played with the toy that had been left on the table. His cold eyes met hers, and she recognized the threat in them.

You wouldn't dare, she thought. Weighing the odds, her chin sunk in defeat. "He's harmless," she lied, willing the tears away. *Yeah, harmless as a water moccasin.*

"Good," Luke replied firmly. He left as quickly as he had

appeared. Rayna trailed after him with more food, leaving her alone with Brent.

The growth of beard on his face made him appear sinister. It was obvious that life as a convict was taking a toll on him. His baby-face was subtly changing to a more hardened, rougher look. He sat back and crossed his arms in satisfaction.

"Thank you," he stated.

Her stomach churned, but she pulled herself together. Raising her chin, she merely humphed as she went to wake Jake from his nap.

Chapter 7

The next afternoon, Emily quietly slipped out of the nursery. Jake was fast asleep, and she was eager for a break. The sight of Rachel in the hall stopped her. It was obvious that she had been waiting.

"I would like for you to join me in the parlor for tea, Miss Emily."

Emily stared at her in shock for a brief second before coming to her senses. "Well," she stammered. "All right. That would be lovely."

She followed the young widow downstairs and sat opposite of her. Watching as her tea was poured for her, she tried not to fidget. After months of servitude, it felt odd to be waited on.

"I brewed the tea just minutes ago. If it's too hot, let me know. I have fresh cream as well," Rachel said, ever the dutiful hostess.

Warily, Emily picked up her cup and saucer. She took a small, testing sip and nodded appreciatively. "This is wonderful, Miss Rachel. Thank you for inviting me."

Rachel blushed becomingly and smoothed a napkin over her lap. "Well, I thought it might be good for you. This must be awfully hard on you, considering you are of genteel stock."

Emily forced herself not to laugh. While it was true that

she had mixed with the upper echelon of New Orleans society, she had never thought of herself as genteel stock. She artfully hid her smile behind her cup as she took another sip.

Rachel waved a gloved hand at her. "Do not forget the pinky."

Emily looked queerly at her. "Excuse me?"

"It's considered polite to extend the pinky while sipping your tea," Rachel instructed.

"Oh," she hesitated, forcing sarcasm away. "I didn't realize that."

"That's all right, Miss Emily. That's why I decided that having afternoon tea would be a great way for you to brush up on your—" Rachel stopped, unsure of how to politely proceed.

"Manners?" Emily offered with a glowering eye.

"Precisely."

Emily was about to set her cup down and take her leave, but the sound of Luke entering the house gave her pause. An idea popped into her head, and she determined to use teatime to her advantage. Try as she might, she could not deny that her heart now belonged to the damnable man, and she wasn't going down without a fight.

Knowing he was within hearing, she smiled superficially and said, quite loudly, "Why, thank you, Miss Rachel. I shall be delighted to suf—I mean, partake of your guidance in the matters of etiquette."

Rachel clapped her gloved hands gleefully, and her face glowed with her accomplishment. "Excellent. Tea shall be at this time every day. That is, if Master Jacob obliges us in napping."

"Well," drawled a male voice. Both females looked toward Luke as his frame filled the parlor doorway. "It's nice to see such a...lovely arrangement."

Although she knew he had heard, Emily pretended otherwise. "Why, Mr. McCabe," she gushed with false femininity. "Miss Rachel has kindly taken me under her wing."

"Oh yes, Lucas," Rachel interrupted, excitement written all over her face. "Isn't it wonderful? I shall guide her in the ways of polite society."

Emily ground her teeth as her eyes sparkled with fire. She knew Rachel was quite aware that she had been raised in the polite society of New Orleans. She wisely bit her tongue to keep from pointing that out.

The amusement on Luke's face, however, told her that he knew exactly what was spinning in her head. It only infuriated her more, but before spiteful words could escape her lips, he spoke.

"That is good news, Rachel. It won't hurt a bit for a brush up on manners."

It was apparent he was having trouble controlling his mirth at Emily's situation. She looked at Rachel with a mischievous twinkle in her eye. "Miss Rachel, wouldn't it be divine if Mr. McCabe joined us?"

Out of the corner of her eye, she noted with satisfaction that his amusement instantly vanished. He proceeded to sputter excuses, but it was Rachel who cut him off this time.

"Oh, that would be lovely. Would you, Lucas?" she pleaded with a flutter of eyelashes. "It would certainly help Emily.

"I...I," he stammered, feeling as trapped as the rabbit he had cornered the other day.

"Please?" Rachel demurely raised innocent eyes. "If business requires, I shall pardon your absence, but please, at least once or twice a week."

"Yes, Mr. McCabe," Emily cooed falsely. "We'd so enjoy your companionship."

Luke's shoulders sagged a touch in defeat. "Alright, la-dies, but only once or twice a week. Most afternoons, I am in the fields."

And so it was settled. Teatime became a daily ritual.

* * * *

A week later, Emily sat on the settee, watching with amusement as Luke fidgeted with the collar at his neck. She recalled the first time he had attempted to take tea with them. The dust on his clothes had sent Rachel into a sneezing fit, and the lady had shooed him out of the room, excusing him until the next day when he could properly wash up.

Rachel quietly cleared her throat. "I was wondering, Lu-cas. Would you mind if I arranged a small gathering of friends next Saturday afternoon?"

Emily watched him inwardly groan and smirked behind her tea cup. Since Rachel's arrival, he was being dragged into society whether he liked it or not. *Oh well,* she thought. *'Twas not I who brought her here.*

"Will I be required to attend?" he asked with a measure of reserve.

Rachel smiled patiently. "Why, of course, dear."

Emily watched his face darken as he hid behind a drink of tea. A moment later, he asked, "What's the occasion?"

"Well," she hesitated, allowing grief to briefly cross her face. "My year of mourning is past, and I thought 'twould be nice..."

"Oh." His face instantly lightened in understanding. "Well, then, I guess it would be alright."

Her face beamed with excitement. "Thank you, Lucas."

Emily carefully watched the exchange, noting with a stab of jealousy that Rachel's hand lingered overly long on Luke's arm. A hint of a smile played at the corners of her mouth.

But has he kissed you like he kissed me? she wondered, as her thoughts carried her back to that life shattering day. *What am I doing? I'm fighting for a man who clearly doesn't want me. Have I gone completely daft?*

"Emily."

She snapped to the present, embarrassed at having been caught daydreaming. She refused, however, to let her cheeks turn red. "I'm sorry, Mr. McCabe. What were you saying?"

The sound of Jake crying upstairs suddenly filled her ears. Luke smiled ruefully. "I think Jake wants you."

Their eyes locked and held, and a familiar fire crackled between them. Her heart filled with sadness at the unbidden words that filled her head. *But do you?*

She jumped to her feet, half afraid he could read her mind. She started toward the baby's room but paused outside the parlor door. Emily threw a parting glance over her shoulder, just in time to see Rachel whisper in Luke's ear. When he turned to look at the widow, she brazenly kissed him.

Emily's heart stopped and tears formed. Biting her lip, she ran up the stairs.

* * * *

Later that night, Emily tossed and turned in her bed. Every time she closed her eyes, she saw Luke and Rachel kissing. Then, when she finally slept, nightmares plagued her.

At first, she was lost in Luke's kiss. Her heart warmed, and she pressed close to him, craving more. Then, he roughly pushed her away and held out his hand. As Rachel placed hers in it, she smiled wickedly at Emily. Luke pulled the widow to him and began to kiss her, not caring if Emily was there or not.

Enraged and hurt, Emily lunged at the couple, only to find they were far out of her reach. She sank to her knees, tears pouring down her face. Instantly awake, she touched her cheek to find it was wet. She sighed wearily and threw back the covers. Deciding sleep was nowhere in sight, she threw on her robe, intent on fetching a cup of tea.

After checking on a sleeping Jake, she quietly opened the door but drew back in alarm. Someone stood in front of Rachel's door. She peeked out, but as it was dark, she couldn't see clearly. The man stood with his back to her while he softly knocked on the widow's door. Her heart shattered as Rachel let him in.

Damn you, Luke, she thought, quickly shutting her own door. *Damn you, damn you, damn you.*

Chapter 8

April 26, 1890
Saturday

Early that morning, a handful of servants arrived. Rachel had hired them to prepare for and serve at the party. Emily stayed in the nursery most of the day, avoiding the pre-party activities. In fact, her intention was to hide there for the next twenty-four hours. After catching Luke and Rachel in a midnight tryst, she couldn't stand the thought of seeing either of them.

Try as she might, though, she couldn't get them off her mind and being cooped up in a room with an infant all day gradually wore on her nerves. So, when the guests began to arrive around four o'clock, she couldn't resist slipping out to see who Rachel's friends were.

With Jake in her arms, she opened the door, jumping at the sight of Brent. Instantly suspicious, she took a step back and glared at him. "What do you want?"

"To talk."

"Where's your guard?"

Brent rolled his eyes. "Waiting at the foot of the stairs, as usual. I led him to believe there was something up here that needed fixing."

The shackles on his feet clanked loudly as he shuffled into the room. He shut the door behind him, and Emily backed up to the open window. The breeze blew the curtain around her head, but she refused to move.

"Touch me, and I'll scream."

He looked at her as if she had lost her mind. "I'm not here for that. Besides, I like my women willing, Emily. You of all people should know that."

"Then what do you want?"

"Tonight is the perfect night to escape."

Emily's mouth fell open. "You cannot be serious."

He towered over her. "Deadly."

Her heart hammered in her chest. Stubbornly, she thrust out her chin. "I don't want any part of this, Brent."

A muscle in his jaw twitched as he silently studied her. "If you don't help me, I'll make sure your new-found lover knows your secret."

She hid the pain that swiftly rose in her heart. "He's not my lover."

Brent snickered. "Come on, Em, I saw the two of you kissing."

"No," she denied. "No one saw us."

"Trust me. I saw, and if you don't cooperate, I'll tell him about our baby. Then we'll see how much he wants you."

Emily closed her eyes as tears formed. "So what? Tell him. He could care less about me anyway."

Her voice caught in her throat as she turned away from him to look out the window. Jake was, for once, quiet in her arms, sensing things were not right.

Brent stepped close, pressing his body against her own. Trapped by the window, she was unable to move away. He put his arms around her waist and whispered seductively in her ear. "Then come away with me."

The door suddenly opened, and both looked to find Rachel staring oddly at them. Brent wisely stepped away, and Emily quickly put more distance between them. Her cheeks flamed, aware of the picture they must have made. Thankfully, Rachel chose to ignore what she had presumably walked in on.

"Miss Emily, I would like a moment of your time, please."

Brent headed out of the room. "I best get back to my chores."

Rachel gave him wide clearance, not bothering to even acknowledge his presence. Once gone, she addressed her charge.

"I find myself one guest short, Miss Emily, and as I've taken the trouble to ensure the number of men equal the number of women, it behooves me to ask for your assistance."

Warily, she asked, "What would you have of me, Miss Rachel?"

"That you join us as my guest."

* * * *

Luckily, Luke's deceased wife was the same size as Emily. Rayna helped her pick out a simple yet beautiful emerald gown from a trunk in the attic. The dust was shaken loose, and Rayna quickly cleaned it as best as possible. Thus, as the last guest arrived at five o'clock, Emily walked down the stairs.

Rachel and Luke stood at the front door, with their backs to her. She noticed the widow had her arm locked to his, and a tremor of jealousy shook through her. Squashing the feeling, she quietly waited behind them. Nervously, she toyed with a lock of her hair.

"Why, Miss Rachel, who is this lovely young lady behind you?" asked a dashing, dark-haired gentleman.

Rachel and Luke turned to look at her. Rachel's eyes widened a bit at how fetching her charge looked, and Luke's eyes darkened with unmistakable fire.

"This is Miss Emily St. Amande, Lord Randolph," Rachel cooed. She grabbed her charge's hand and pulled her forward. "And your dinner partner."

His brown eyes glittered like a snake's as he took her hand and pressed it to his lips. "My pleasure."

"Well, I do believe that everyone is in the dining room," Rachel stated. "Shall we join them?"

Emily boldly glanced at Luke, feeling his eyes on her. He wore his sour face, and she felt certain it had something to do with her.

Hmpf, she thought. *He will just have to deal with my presence. It's not like I invited myself to this little soirée.*

Lifting her chin, she allowed Lord Randolph to escort her in, determined to ignore Luke McCabe as much as possible, despite the fact that his handsomeness took her breath away.

* * * *

"Five smelly crawfish, four slimy bass, three cypress trees, two of Pierre's pirogues and a big fat alligator," Rachel smiled proudly.

After eating, the party of fourteen had moved to the ball-room to partake of a few parlor games. At the moment, they were in the midst of the Game of Ten, whereas each item must be repeated exactly as stated or the player is removed from the game.

The players had whittled down to Rachel, Luke, Emily and Lord Randolph. The remaining ten guests watched on in amusement. The game would continue until there were no more players.

Wondering how he had gotten himself mixed up in parlor activities, Luke nonetheless complied. "Six nasty rats, five smelly crawfish, four slimy bass, three cypress trees, two of Pierre's pirogues and..." he paused, acting as if he couldn't remember. "A big...fat alligator."

He then looked at Emily, and the heat of his gaze melted every part of her body. "I believe it's your turn, Miss Emily."

She swallowed, and after adding seven deceitful snakes, correctly recited the phrase. Lord Randolph patted her knee with improper familiarity. Oddly, no one seemed to notice or care.

"Well done, Miss Emily, well done. Now," he said. "Let's see, what shall I add? Oh yes, I've got it. Eight breeding bunnies, seven deceitful snakes, six nasty rats, five slimy crawfish—"

Rachel held up a sky-blue gloved hand and waved her finger in the air. "No-no-no, Lord Randolph. I believe that it is five smelly crawfish."

His brow crinkled as he thought. "Are you sure?"

The phrase keeper stood and confirmed the list. Rachel laughed. "Quite sure. You, sir, have been removed from the game."

Rather sadly, he moved his chair back out of the circle, and the three remaining players drew closer together. Rachel clasped her hands under her chin. "Let's see."

She chewed her lip thoughtfully, loving that the attention was on her. Past experience lent a hand as she drew out the intensity of the game by stating each phrase slowly and with great concentration.

"Nine captured doves."

Emily's eyes widened a bit at the words. The blue eyes staring so intently at her held a glint of malice, but for the life of her, she could not fathom why Rachel was suddenly acting so spiteful towards her.

"Eight breeding bunnies," she laughed, as thoughts turned

sinful. "Seven deceitful snakes, six needy rats—"

Emily smiled coldly. "Wrong."

Rachel instantly realized her mistake and pouted prettily. "Drat."

She stood and moved her chair back from the circle but not much farther from Luke's side. The remaining two were forced to face one another, and Emily felt it a bit disconcerting that the barest touch of his knees against hers blazed with heat.

The room fell away as he smiled charmingly at her. "Ten frolicking foals."

A remembered kiss suddenly surface, and her cheeks flushed. He then correctly rattled off the rest of the phrase, and she, in turn, did the same. The room burst into conversation as Rachel slowly stood.

"It seems we have a tie, then," she stated loudly and looked about. "How shall we break it?"

"A game of cards," suggested Lord Randolph.

"How about charades?" asked Molly, one of the twins.

"Tableaux vivant," one of the men said.

Emily's blood ran cold.

Chapter 9

"Perfect," cried out a female voice.

The room buzzed with talk, and Emily silently groaned. She looked at Rachel, amazed at the displeasure on her face.

"I say a card game," Rachel stammered weakly.

"Nonsense, Rachel. Living statues will be perfect," Molly stated. "The first one who moves loses, but they can make faces. And to add further distraction, we shall all dance around them."

The next thing Emily knew, she was standing nose to nose with Luke, or rather, her nose to his chin. Molly and her twin sister had taken charge of the posing. Out of the corner of her eye, she saw a hint of outrage on Rachel's face.

They placed them as if they were dancing, with his hands on her waist and hers on his shoulders. Then, to make it harder, they tilted up her chin so that she had to look into his face.

"Don't move," ordered Molly and left them alone in the center of the room.

Someone began to play the piano, and everyone began to dance around the 'statues'. Molly, however, stood close by and watched for movement.

"This is ridiculous," Luke muttered through clenched teeth.

Emily made no reply, trying to keep still. Her heart beat in her chest like the captured dove Rachel had mentioned. All she could think of was his hands on her waist. She avoided looking into his eyes, concentrating instead on the way his soft brown hair fell away from his face.

This is not working, she thought, wondering how it felt to run her fingers through it. Her hands itched to feel its softness. Nervously, she swallowed, reminding herself that he had kissed Rachel as well as visited her in the middle of the night.

"This is ridiculous," he muttered again.

Irritated, she replied through slightly parted lips, "Then 'ove."

His competitiveness rose to the forefront. "No."

Rising to the challenge, she felt compelled to cross her eyes in an attempt to make him smile. The corners of his mouth lifted slightly, but he managed to hold his composure. She did it once more, but it made her dizzy.

Meanwhile, couples would stop every now and then to inspect them. All were amazed that they were still in position. Several waved their hands in front of their faces in an attempt to jolt them into movement, but they had indeed turned into living statues. Neither wanted to give in.

"My muscles ache," Luke whispered through gritted teeth.

"Then move."

"Not on your life, darling."

All of a sudden, a dancing couple ran into Emily, knocking her against him. No one but Molly seemed to notice, as they had been still for so long. The twin threw her hands up in aggravation and proceeded to chastise the drunken couple.

Luke's arms wrapped around Emily to keep her from falling, and so she found herself nestled against his chest. The feeling of completeness enveloped her once more, and she sighed, noticing that he briefly hesitated before letting her go.

"Oh well," he laughed. "I lost."

He stepped back from her, making a grand show of being a sporting loser when technically, she had moved first. Rachel quickly claimed his arm as Lord Randolph pressed a glass of lemonade into Emily's hand.

"You must be parched," he said, leading her to a nearby chair.

She nodded, and as she drank, she scanned the room. Luke sat on the opposite side with Rachel fussing over him. He raised his head and smoldering brown eyes met hers. Her heart broke at the thought that he would never be hers.

"I need fresh air," she whispered.

Lord Randolph jumped to his feet and held out his hand. "Why, certainly, my dear."

* * * *

Emily leaned against the porch rail and stared at the half moon. She closed her eyes and breathed in deeply, smelling the honeysuckle that perfumed the air. With every ounce of her soul, she longed to be by Luke's side.

"Are you feeling well, Miss Emily?"

She turned her head and looked at the dark-haired gentleman beside her. She faked a most charming smile. "Yes, I feel better now. Thank you."

He slipped his arm about her waist and pulled her close to him. Then, without bothering to ask, he kissed her, running his hands over places he had no right to. She pushed against his chest, but he only tightened his embrace. So, she slyly snaked her hand up his neck and yanked his ear as hard as she could.

Pain overwhelmed his lustful attack, and he stepped back in shock. She took the opportunity. Balling up her fist, she pulled back her arm and hit him as hard as she could in the jaw. Unfortunately, it hardly fazed him and sent a shower of pain through her hand. Tears sprang to her eyes, and she cradled the injured hand under her arm.

"Well, that was a damn stupid thing to do," Lord Randolph responded. He stepped closer to her and whispered, "But if it's what you like..."

"Stop," she said frantically, backing up. "I don't—"

"What's going on here?"

Both Emily and Lord Randolph looked toward the house. Luke stood in the doorway, his hands still holding the doorknob. She couldn't see his face, but she sensed an inner rage.

"Why, the little jailbird came onto me," Lord Randolph sputtered. "And when I wouldn't give her what she wanted, she punched me."

He then touched his jaw as if it actually hurt. "I think I need some ice."

Emily's face screwed up in disbelief. "That's a lie. He came on to me."

Luke stepped out onto the porch and quietly shut the doors. He gently took Emily's arm and pulled her behind him. "I think, sir, that you should see to your ice..." he hesitated. "Before I make sure you need a steak instead."

Emily's heart suddenly welled up with unwanted love. He had taken her side. Some part of him certainly cared for her.

A brief battle of wills ensued between the men. Then, Lord Randolph turned on his heel and hurried inside. *He doesn't want his pretty-boy features messed up for some convict,* she thought wryly.

Luke turned his attention to her hand. She winced as he gently pulled her fingers out. The skin on each knuckle was red and scraped. He turned her hand up and lightly ran his fingers over her sensitive skin. She shivered and watched in shock as he raised her palm to his lips. A jolt of desire rippled through her. She stifled a whimper that rose in her throat. As if coming to his senses, he let go of her hand and took one step back.

"I shouldn't have done that."

"I believe you've already used that bit before," Emily replied quietly.

He motioned to the door. "Please. We can't do this."

The pain rose just as quickly as desire had. "No," she answered haughtily. "I suppose Rachel wouldn't like it one bit."

Lifting her chin, she hurried inside without waiting for him.

* * * *

Thankfully, no one noticed as Emily ran past the ballroom and up the stairs. It was late. She was tired and fed up with Luke's shenanigans. Pausing at the top of the stairs, she counted on her fingers the months left of servitude. Her shoulders sagged. Ten months was an awful long time.

Perhaps I may ask to be moved to a different plantation, she thought, heading for her room.

She almost screamed as she rounded a corner and ran into someone. That person, however, quickly grabbed her and covered her mouth.

"Shhh," Brent growled.

She pushed at his shoulders, surprised when he released her. "You idiot."

"It's time," he whispered.

She shook her head. "Oh, no. I'll not be a fugitive for you as well. You got me into this mess—"

"Then let me get you out," he pleaded.

"No."

Sighing, he reluctantly pulled out a revolver and pointed it at her. "I think yes."

Emily placed her hands on her hips and looked at him as if

he'd lost his mind. "You can just shoot me, then, cause I'm not going. I won't be hunted down like a deer."

"Damn it, woman," Brent struggled to keep from shouting. "What the hell do you know about being incarcerated? You've been set up in this nice house since you got here."

"Where are you going to go, Brent?" Emily countered. "You'll be a fugitive for the rest of your life. How much longer do you have?"

He hesitated before replying. "One year and eleven months."

"If you escape, you'll be in prison the rest of your life as you will always be looking over your shoulder for the authorities. Not to mention, if you are caught, years will be added to your sentence."

He frowned and lowered the revolver. "I hate it here."

She placed a hand on his. "So do I."

He eyed her fancy dress. "I can see that."

She rolled her eyes. "Trust me. I hate it here. Now please put that revolver back in Mr. McCabe's cabinet."

He smiled sheepishly. "It wasn't loaded anyway."

Chapter 10

June 30, 1890

As the months passed, Emily and Rachel settled into an unnatural, forced relationship. Every time Emily turned around, Rachel was chastising her for inappropriate and unladylike behavior. Somehow, it only encouraged Emily to torment her more.

The woman even had the nerve to impose on her dining habits, although she still partook of her meals in the kitchen with Rayna and Brent. For instance, if she were caught eating meat with her salad fork, she was scolded immediately with no heed for whoever else was in the room. The minute Rachel left, Brent would burst into laughter, sorely tempting Emily to throw the salad fork at him.

This afternoon, Emily was desperately trying not to brood. She missed Luke and how he used to appear out of nowhere and whisk her off to see some amazing miracle that was happening on the plantation.

Fortunately, Jake was proving to be a delightful distraction, and they sat on the floorboards of the porch. She held his tiny hands as he pulled himself up into a standing position.

"That's good, Jake," Emily cooed. "You're doing great."

The screen door opened, and Rayna stuck her head out.

"Miss Rachel say it's tea time."

Emily groaned. "Oh joy."

Rayna smiled. "I tell her you say that."

Emily gave her a friendly glare. "Do, and I'll tell her where you hide your cigarettes."

"Oh, you no fun."

Emily sighed. "Ok, I'm coming."

Wearily, she got to her feet. Jake raised his arms to be picked up. "Oh, don't worry, little one. You're invited, too. It's never too early to learn your manners."

A snort of laughter caused her to turn around. Brent peered at her over the hedges. "Guess you need three or four tea times a day."

"You know, Brent, you could use a good eyebrow pluck-ing three or four times a day."

She smiled as his hand self-consciously touched his brow. Raising her chin, she turned on her heel and left him to pon-der his facial hair.

* * * *

While Jake played with his portion of bread and butter on the parlor floor, the two women daintily sipped their tea. Emily furtively watched the unusually quiet Rachel, who seemed to be in another world.

"Are we not feeling well, Miss Rachel?"

The widow jumped, and her cheeks flamed guiltily. "Oh my. I am sorry, Miss Emily." She popped open her fan and waved it over her flushed skin. "I seem to be out of sorts."

Anxious to escape, Emily started to set her cup down. "Then perhaps you should take a nap."

"Oh, dear me, no. I...I'd rather not be alone at the mo-ment."

Emily's ears perked as she sensed the widow's distress, and although she should have minded her own, she couldn't resist butting her nose in where it probably didn't belong. "What's wrong?"

Rachel's worried eyes met Emily's. Then she glanced around to make sure they were alone and dipped her head in shame. "I...I fear I am with child," she whispered.

Emily nearly dropped the cup as her heart lodged in her throat. The thought of Luke and Rachel making love brought tears to her eyes, but she closed them briefly and willed them away.

"God is punishing me," the widow cried as tears streamed down her face.

Not knowing what else to do, Emily awkwardly reached over and placed a hand over Rachel's. "Shhh, don't cry. 'Twill be alright. Are you positive?"

"I'm as regular as the sun, and I am late by two weeks." Rachel frowned, sniffing.

Although her chaperon was older by two years, Emily felt the elder at the moment. "Have you seen a doctor?"

Blonde ringlets shook negatively. "I'm frightened. My reputation—"

Emily rolled her eyes. "To hell with what other people say." She hesitated, swallowing over the lump in her throat at the thought of her next question. "Have you told Lu—uh, Mr. McCabe?"

At this, the widow burst into fresh tears. "I can't. I can't."

"Can't what?"

The sight of Luke standing in the doorway sent Rachel into a fainting spell. Emily glared at the dust-covered man. Her thoughts spun in a million different directions as she watched him race to Rachel's side. He gathered the unconscious woman in his arms and headed toward the upstairs.

"You son-of-a-bitch," she growled.

He stopped and looked over his shoulder. "What?" he asked, half angry, half perplexed.

"At first, I thought it was your dead wife that kept us from being together," she whispered, close to tears. She thrust up her chin. "But now I see 'tis not the case. I see the demands of society does hold reign over you to some extent but not very far."

"What the hell are you talking about?"

Emily pointed at Rachel. "Your *lady* is pregnant."

* * * *

With crossed arms, Emily waited impatiently outside Rachel's room as Luke laid the unconscious widow on her bed. Then he left Rayna to care for her and stepped out into the hall, quietly closing the door behind him. Emily watched his face anxiously, torn between wanting to scratch his eyes out and wanting to run away and cry.

He closed the space between them and gently grabbed her shoulders. She jerked at his touch, but he held her firmly. He searched her eyes imploringly.

"I'm not the father, Emily."

She snorted and focused on the opposite wall. "What do I care? I'm just a convict."

Before she could react, Luke captured her lips in a deep, demanding kiss. She struggled, but he refused to let her go. Instead, he wrapped his arms around her and pulled her tightly against him. As the kiss continued, the ice in her veins melted, and she suddenly realized her hands had slipped around his neck. Her fingers sunk into soft hair, and the intensity of his kiss tilted her world.

Minutes later, he pulled back, and his look sent warmth through her body. "I have tried to get you out of my head, Emily. I have tried damn hard," he whispered huskily. "And when Rachel arrived, I had hoped...well, anyway, she can't hold a candle to you."

Once again, he kissed her, shaking her soul and leaving her thoughtless. When they pulled apart, it was a complete surprise to see Brent standing right beside them. They both jumped guiltily away from each other. Brent merely shook his head and managed to look hurt.

"I thought you loved me, Emily," he stated in a strangled voice. "The other night, you swore you loved only me."

The innocence on his face belied the treachery in his eyes, and Emily choked on the sudden fear that rose in her. She looked at Luke, shaking her head. "I don't know what he's talking about."

"Oh, come on, Em," Brent implored. "I know I promised to take care of you last year after you lost our child, and I swear that after we're set free—"

"Wait, back up." Luke held up his hand to Brent. Emily's face paled, and she felt near to fainting herself when he focused on her. "What is he talking about, Emily? Did you have relations with him?"

"She still is," Brent stated proudly.

Words stuck in her throat as she shook her head in denial. Her blood pounded in her ears, and she closed her eyes. *This is not happening. He is not there. He is not ruining this.*

"Emily?" Luke demanded. "Did you carry his child?"

A single tear slipped down her cheek as she opened her eyes. She bravely thrust up her chin. "Yes, but I lost it."

Chapter 11

"Oh no."

A voice from the doorway had everyone's head turning, and the sight of Rachel holding tightly to the frame had Luke rushing to her side. Emily masked the pain of watching his gallantry. She turned to leave, but the widow's words stopped her from fleeing the scene.

"I'm such a fool," Rachel whispered. Her eyes were fixed on Brent's face. Pulling herself together, she drew herself up proudly and quickly closed the space between them. The loud smack of her hand on his cheek rang in everyone's ears. "That's for lying to me."

She raised her hand to hit him again, but Luke grabbed it from behind. Her face turned red with rage, and she turned on Luke. "Let me go. He deserves another for impregnating me."

Luke's upper lip twitched as he suppressed a sneer. "Did he take you without your consent?"

A bit taken back, Rachel stammered, "Why, no, of course not."

"Then you consented to having relations with him."

The blonde's heart shaped face turned a deeper, more embarrassed shade of red. "Yes," she replied meekly.

Luke released her arm. "Then he is not entirely at fault,

Miss Rachel."

Then he turned to Brent. "Well," he drawled. "It seems you're making the rounds."

At this, Emily exploded. "He's not making any rounds with me."

Luke raised his eyebrow. "But—"

Emily cut him off. "That was then. This is now, and frankly, I don't give a damn what you think about me anymore."

The sound of Jake crying gave her an opportunity to escape. She started to go to the child, but Luke grabbed her arm. "Oh, no, Miss Emily. I don't think so."

He hollered for Rayna, and when the squaw appeared, he gave her instructions to watch the child. He then indicated for everyone to enter Rachel's room. "I suggest we continue this in private and not in the hall."

Rather reluctantly, they entered the room. Emily stood by the window and twisted her hair. Rachel flopped onto the bed and began to bite her nails. Brent stood in a corner with his arms crossed, and Luke blocked the door.

"Let me get this straight. You and Rachel now."

Brent nodded solemnly. "Yes, sir."

"And you and Emily a year ago."

"One time," Emily spat vehemently. "Big mistake."

Luke glanced a warning at her briefly before directing his attention back to Brent. "But you just got through saying, or rather, implying that you and Emily are now having relations. So which is it, Brent? Are you now having relations with Miss Emily?"

A heavy silence permeated the room as everyone waited for his answer. Brent glanced from one woman to the other, feeling the weight of their malevolent stare. He took a deep breath and let it out slowly. "No, sir. I am not."

Luke lost it. "Then why the hell did you imply that you were?"

Brent shrugged. "I don't know, sir. Maybe, I guess, I was jealous."

"Jealous of what, Brent?"

A muscle in his jaw twitched, and he looked at the floor. "Of the way that you look at her. Of the fact that she loves you and not me anymore."

Emily's anger turned to shock, and her heart dropped to the floor. "Brent!"

"Oh, come on, Em. You know it's true." He choked on his next words. "It's a bitter pill realizing what you've lost too late."

Luke remained quiet as the information sunk in. His face, however, no longer held the look of a tornado ready to form. He desperately wished he had something to chew on.

"Well," he drawled. "I know you come from a good family, Brent. I check out the history of every convict on this plantation, and while you still have a year and a half left of your sentence, I think it would be in everybody's best interest if you and Miss Rachel were married."

At this, Rachel gasped. "I can't marry a convict."

Luke turned and looked at her with a glare in his eye. "But you can spread your legs for one?"

Her eyes widened at the rudeness of his words. "How dare you."

"I think, Miss Rachel, your reputation is far beyond repair, and you're not going to blame this child on me. Now, I'll do what I can to see Brent released a little bit early, and after that, I'll even offer him a regular job on this plantation, if he wants it." He stated his next words firm and clear. "But you will marry him."

With that said, he held out his hand to Emily. "I think we

should leave these two to talk, Miss Emily. Besides, I'd like a word with you in private."

* * * *

The rain beat angrily against the house, and gusts of wind blew sporadically across the porch. Emily sat on the swing, furtively watching Luke. He stood looking out toward the road with one hand on the post and a foot on the bottom of the porch rail. She shivered as the cold feeling of change touched her soul.

"I expect this rain'll be here for a few days," he said. "It's about time, though."

Emily looked at her hands, wishing he'd quit dragging his feet. Tired of the torment, she spoke. "I'm sorry I didn't tell you about the baby."

He looked at her curiously. "Sorry for what? That's personal business. You don't have to tell me a damn thing."

"My father doesn't even know about it," she continued. "I only carried it for two months."

He leaned against the rail. His face was open and sincere. "You come with a past. So what? I have a past. I've done things I'm not so proud of. The question is, did you learn?"

Emily snorted. "Did I ever."

"Well there ya go."

He pushed away from the rail and offered his hand. "I know it's raining, but I have to show you something."

* * * *

Miss Rachel will really be upset now, Emily thought as the rain dripped over the bright blue parasol. The fabric was ruined; it was only meant to be used as sunshade. She made a face when she stepped in a puddle, and the cold water soaked through her boots to her toes.

"I'm sorry. I'll buy you another pair," Luke said, noticing her distress.

She made no reply as a sudden whip of wind tried to carry the parasol away. While he wasn't under it, he grabbed it and held it firmly. His wet arm dripped on the bodice of her dress. At the moment, she wanted distance between them.

"It's alright. I have it."

Relinquishing his hold, he took a step forward and placed his hand on the tombstone. "Miss Emily, I'd like you to meet my wife."

He closed his eyes briefly, reminding himself that she was gone. "I mean, this is where Sarah rests."

Feeling awkward, she watched the rain run down his face. He hadn't shaved in a day and already there was stubble on his chin. He had been working in the stable as the rain prevented work in the fields, and he still wore his work clothes. As it was hot, there were no sleeves on his shirt, and his biceps bulged. She forced herself to look at the grave.

She smiled wryly. "Nice to meet you, Sarah."

"Well," he drawled. "Today seems to be a day of truths."

Emily placed a hand on her hip. "Please, I daresay I have had enough of truth. I know you're still in love with your wife."

"Would you let me finish?" he asked in exasperation.

She inclined her head. "If you must."

He chewed on his lower lip, trying to choose his words carefully. "My mother died in childbirth when I was ten. My baby sister went with her. My father died when I was thirteen, and I came to live here with my uncle Owen. He was killed in the fields when I was twenty, and as his closest relative, I inherited all of this. So, I'm well acquainted with Death."

Luke paused, licking the rain off his lips. "I learned early how short our time on earth is, and so I set about finding a wife. With the help of a close business associate, I dove right into Baton Rouge society. I would have drowned had I not met Sarah."

He moved away from the headstone and sat on a nearby stone bench. He crossed his arms. "She fell in love with me, and so I married her. I loved her deeply."

Luke hung his head, ashamed of his truth. "But I gotta tell you. I was never in love with her, and there's a difference. I married her to continue on with my line. We were better friends than lovers."

He shrugged. "So we settled into a comfortable almost platonic relationship. It's a wonder Jake was ever conceived."

Emily's heart sped up, and she took a step toward him. A loud crash behind her made her turn around. A rather large tree limb had fallen directly in the spot where she had been standing. Her eyes widened, and she jumped further away as if the limb would come to life.

"Oh my God."

In an instant, Luke was behind her. He placed his hands on her shoulders and pulled her close. "Are you okay?"

Numbly, she nodded. "Just a bit unnerved."

"The weather's getting worse. I think we should head back."

She twisted around in his arms. His face was temptingly close, and she unconsciously licked her lips. "Wait. Please. I want you to finish."

He searched her face as feelings he'd never experienced rushed through him. His heart swelled at the look of innocence in her eyes. She always tried to hide it with her sauciness, which was one of the reasons he found himself attracted to her.

"I love you, Emily."

A smile twitched at her mouth, but she forced it away. "But are you *in* love with me?"

He didn't have a chance to reply. A flash of lightening and a loud clap of thunder had them running for cover. She dropped the parasol in favor of picking up her skirts. She glanced back to make sure he was there. Unfortunately, she stepped in hole at the same time and fell head first into a tree, knocking herself unconscious.

* * * *

"Please open your eyes, Emily. Please."

Reluctantly, she obeyed the pleading voice. Luke's worried face hovered inches from hers, and she realized she was in his arms. They were still in the woods, under a huge tree that partially blocked the rain.

She watched as relief washed over his face, welcoming his warm kiss. Her arms wound around his neck, and her fingers sunk into wet hair. Closing her eyes, she lost herself in his embrace.

He blazed kisses all over her face and neck and then proceeded to nuzzle her breasts. Minutes later, he came to his senses and seized his ravaging of her body.

"I'm sorry. I shouldn't have."

She couldn't help but laugh. "Your favorite line."

"I'm serious."

Her smile faded. "You haven't answered my question."

He searched her eyes. "I swore I'd never marry again unless I was in love."

She held her breath, forcing her mouth shut. She wasn't going to ruin this moment with her comments. He kissed her again, and the softness of his assault melted her insides. He pressed his warm lips to her ear.

"Will you marry me?"

Chapter 12

Emily didn't care that she was drenched. She climbed the stairs with a smile on her face and a song in her heart. Luke had asked her to marry him. Nothing else mattered.

She entered her bedroom, musing on how much she had changed since her arrival. Her former self would have balked at marrying any man, much less a farm boy from Baton Rouge. She never thought she could feel so good.

Emily placed her hands on the baby's bedrail and fondly watched him sleep. She determined then and there to do her best by Luke and Jake and would not die on them. She was sure of that to the bottom of her soul. God had sent her here, and here she would stay.

Suddenly, a big, smelly hand covered her mouth, and the cold tip of a gun rested against her temple. Her eyes widened in surprise, but that only lasted a second. She narrowed them in aggravation.

"Brent," she growled against the grimy palm. Her hands wrapped around the thick wrist as she attempted to remove his hand. "For the last time, I am not running away with you."

"Shut up," ordered an unfamiliar voice. Emily tensed, instantly realizing she was mistaken. Real terror gripped her heart. She waited for the man to make his intentions known.

"Pick up the brat and make sure he doesn't squall."

She did as she was told. Jake whimpered but did not wake. Her brows drew together as she wondered what the stranger wanted. Alarm ran through her at the sound of a match striking, and she watched helplessly as the man threw the flaming stick into Jake's baby bed. It ignited instantly, and flames began licking at the walls.

The man pulled her towards the door, and she saw his face for the first time. She had no idea as to who he was. The tip of his finger touched his long, crooked nose as he motioned for her silence. A scar ran from his cheek to his chin. A cowboy hat covered his eyes, but she knew she was better off not seeing the hate in them. He pointed the gun at Jake.

"Not a sound."

They managed to get out of the house without a single soul seeing them. She pulled the blanket over Jake's head to keep off the cold rain. The man pushed her down the driveway, making her practically run. They were almost to the road when she heard the screams coming from the house. She turned to look, but the man shoved her forward.

"Keep going."

"But they'll think we're in there."

"Good," he grunted and shoved her again.

Her heart ached for the torment Luke would go through. She couldn't bear the thought, and she ran forward as fast as she could in an effort to escape. Unfortunately, the man easily caught up and grabbed a fistful of her hair. Her head jerked back, and her feet flew out from under her. She landed on her rump, and Jacob woke up screaming. A carriage then rolled to a stop in front of them, and the door flew open. The man pulled on her hair, forcing her to her feet.

"Get in," he yelled.

She reluctantly obliged and tried to calm the boy as the carriage began to move. She glared at the man seated across from her. She was wary of the gun but not scared. If he was going to kill them, he'd have done it already.

"Who are you?" she demanded.

He sneered. "I'm the foreman he fired."

* * * *

Jake clung to Emily as the pirogue glided through the bayou. Thankfully, the rain had stopped just as they were getting into the small boat. The moon was hidden by the clouds, and the only light came from the lanterns. Two other men had joined them, but all pretty much refused to speak to her. It was just as well. She had nothing to say that would do her or Jake any good.

An owl hooted eerily, and the bullfrogs bellowed. She wondered how many snakes and alligators they had passed. She tightened her arms around Jake and buried her face in his small shoulder. Her heart burned at the thought of Luke. He must think them to be dead. He wouldn't know to go looking for them. So she would just have to find a way to escape.

About thirty minutes later, they arrived at their destination. Set back deep in the swamp was a rundown shack. They tied the pirogue to the pier and crossed the small strip of land. She worried the whole time that she would step on a snake or something worse.

Wordlessly, they marched her through the front door, across the small dirty living room and into a small bedroom. Then they shut and locked the door without leaving a light. She banged on the wood.

"How rude. We can't even see."

Jake had started wailing. He had always been frightened of the dark. There had always been a light in the nursery. Now, Emily couldn't even see her hand. Who knew what creepy crawlies they were expected to bed with.

She slammed her fist against the middle of the door. "Hey, I'm not going to stop until you give us some light."

She pounded some more to emphasize her point, and the door was suddenly flung open. The fired foreman angrily shoved a lantern in her face.

"What about food? Did you even think to bring milk for Jacob?"

"Can't you wet nurse him?"

She gave him a droll stare as she pointed to her chest. "Do these look like they have milk in them?"

After staring at her small breasts, he pursed his lips and nodded in agreement. "Good point. He'll have to drink water until we can get some."

He started to shut the door, but she stopped it with her foot. "When are you going to let us go?"

He gave her a calculated once over look. "Yer welcome to leave anytime you like...but the brat stays with me."

He reached out and tousled the boy's dark hair. "He's my son now."

* * * *

Emily picked at the stuffing that poked out of the arm of the couch. The material was stained and torn and had a vile smell. It was, however, free of bugs, making it one less thing for her to worry about.

Her temples throbbed, and she rested her forehead in the palm of her hand. It had been a week, and the foreman had yet to leave her and Jake alone. The man's chair forever blocked the front door, which was the only exit out of the God forsaken shack.

She had been allowed to go outside, but never with Jacob. At her insistence that the child get fresh air, the foreman began taking him out. But she had to remain inside.

At the moment, the boy was playing on the floor with a toy the foreman had carved out of wood for him. The man continuously gave him treats and toys, seeking to become Jake's father figure. Emily saw through the man's antics, and it depressed her. She feared if she left to go seek Luke, that the man would spirit Jake to another hiding place. She refused to let that happen.

"Memmi."

Jake patted her knee. She looked at his sweet baby face. His little fingers drummed on her leg. She tried to smile.

"Yes, honey?"

"Dada."

Her heart broke, and she forced back the tears. She scooped him into her lap. "Oh, Jake, Dada not coming."

He pointed behind her. "Dada."

Hope surged through her as she turned around. It shattered just as quickly when she saw nothing in the window. She sighed despondently.

"No. Dada at home. He doesn't know we're even alive."

He patted her shoulder and looked at the foreman. "Dada."

Her breath caught in her chest. It had only been a week. Surely he hadn't forgotten Luke so soon. "No, he is NOT Dada."

The boy frowned and began to bounce on her lap. His whining turned to a screaming fit. He slid off her lap and ran towards the foreman, but at the last second, he darted into the kitchen.

Emily jumped off the couch and ran after him. "Jacob McCabe, you come here this instant."

The back of a hand came out of nowhere and hit her square in the eye. It knocked her to the floor. Stunned, she looked up at the foreman. He towered over her menacingly with his face twisted in rage.

"Carter," he spat. "The boy's name is Jacob Carter."

He pointed his whittling knife at her. "Ye'll do well to remember it."

He then stepped away and turned his back on her. "Now go tend to the brat."

Her fingers tenderly touched her throbbing cheek. When she looked at her fingertips, she saw blood. She bit back the tears and stuck her nose in the air. She slowly got to her feet and headed for the kitchen. She was shoved from behind, and she stumbled into the kitchen.

"Hurry up. No telling what he's gotten into."

Her shock was quickly replaced with anger. She had taken orders from everyone for the past four months. She had had enough. Her Irish temper rose, and she slowly faced the foreman.

"Don't ever touch me again," she said with clenched teeth.

His eyes glittered like a snake's, and his tongue darted at the corners of his mouth. His hands clenched as he closed the distance between them. She stood her ground despite the fear. She stared defiantly into his evil eyes.

Before she realized what he was doing, his hands gripped her upper arms, and his fingers dug painfully into her flesh. His rancid breath gagged her as he stole a kiss. She then came to life and fought like a tigress.

Her foot stomped on his, and she scratched his forearms. Still, he would not set her mouth free. Just as she was about to pass out from lack of air, she raised her knee and knocked him hard in the groin. He let go of her with a cry of pain. As he sank to the floor, she raced into the kitchen.

Jake played innocently with a spoon and bowl while she threw open drawers in search of a knife. When she thought all hope was lost, she found a small one. Grunting triumphantly, she started to turn around but a blow to the side of her head stopped her cold. The small knife was ripped from her hand, and she received the beating of her life. Hate truly entered her heart for the first time, and before sinking into unconsciousness, she swore revenge would be sweet.

Chapter 13

Emily moaned and tried to move. She was so stiff and couldn't remember why. Of course, it all rushed back to her when she opened her eyes. She was on the floor of the bedroom she shared with Jake. Carter knelt above her with his pants unbuckled and a lustful sneer on his face. Panicking, she tried to slither out from under him, but his knees were on her dress. She balled up her fist and hit his chin as hard as she could. Then she dug her fingernails into his cheeks.

He hollered in pain and somehow managed to grab her flailing hands. She was trapped, and she turned her head to the side. A single tear slipped out and slid down her bruised and split cheek. She focused on Jake crying in the doorway.

"Not in front of the child," she begged.

Carter looked to the door, realizing for the first time that Jake was there. "Get out of here, you dumb brat."

To emphasize, he let go of Emily's hands, pulled off his shoe and threw it at the boy. It hit him in the stomach, and the poor child commenced to crying even harder. Enraged and free, Emily took the opportunity to sit up. She lunged at Carter, catching him at the right time and knocked him over. As luck would have it, his head hit the sharp corner of the dresser. He went down like a sack of potatoes.

Wasting no time, Emily jumped to her feet, grabbed Jake

and ran out of the shack. The other men were off hunting, and they had taken the pirogue. She looked about frantically before running around to the back of the shack.

She faced the thick swamp, knowing it was the only choice she had. Or was it? She paused and looked at Jake. A swamp was no place for a baby. They'd never make it.

She looked back at the house. Her mind set, she pulled a shovel out of the shed. There was nowhere to hide Jake, so she reluctantly brought him back to the front porch. She sat him on the bottom step and pressed her forehead to his.

"For God's sake, Jacob. Please don't move. I'll be right back. There's something I have to take care of."

Then she silently re-entered the shack with the shovel poised over her shoulder. Her blood hammered through her veins as she approached the bedroom. She heard muffled grunts and groans and quickened her pace before Carter woke. She was one step away from the door, however, when Carter sailed through it.

Luke then appeared in the doorway and hesitated as he saw her bruised and bloodied face. His eyebrows furrowed, and his mouth turned down. He actually growled before going after the foreman. His hesitation, however, cost him the upper hand. Carter had put the couch between them.

Luke started to step on the cushions, intent on going over it. He stopped when Carter pulled out the whittling knife. Luke held out his right hand to Emily.

"Shovel," he spat.

She had already taken a step toward him with the shovel's handle extended to him, and she placed it in his hand at the same time he requested it. He swung it at Carter. The man ducked and came up swinging the knife. He sliced the underside of Luke's arm. The shovel flew across the room as his fingers lost their strength. He stumbled back holding his injured arm. A fiery rage burned in his eyes.

"Get out, Em," he ordered, backing up toward the door.

Carter threw the knife at Luke. It sailed past him and landed in Emily's left shoulder. Shocked, she exchanged a horrified look with Luke before sinking to her knees.

The blade ate at her flesh, sending flames through her veins. Her fingers encircled the hilt, but Luke stopped her before she could pull it out. Sweat beaded on her forehead as her vision started to swim.

A shadow fell across her and she looked at the figure in the front doorway. Brent aimed and fired the shotgun without hesitation. She heard Carter cry out and then heard his body hit the floor.

She looked to Luke and sagged in his arms. His big hands shook. She took a deep breath and said through clenched teeth, "I am not dying. Do you hear me?"

Her tone softened at the worry in his eyes. She smiled and touched his stubbled cheek. "I promise."

Her body relaxed into a state of unconsciousness.

* * * *

"How did you know where to find us?" Emily asked.

She was tucked in bed good and tight. Per the doctor's orders, she was to have bed rest for one week, and then she could rise. The knife had missed major organs and bones but had gone deep. Her muscles would be sore for months.

Luke sat beside her on a chair. "As luck would have it, one of the other guards came to me and told me. Carter had even taken the man there once on a fishing trip."

Emily rolled her eyes. "Wow, Carter was *really* smart, but I'm glad to see you caught the fire before it spread to the rest of the house."

The corners of his mouth turned down. "I must have just missed y'all. I was coming up to check on Jake when I smelled the smoke. God only knows how, but only his room was damaged."

She smiled weakly and winced as she tried to get comfortable. Luke jumped up and started fussing over her like an old mother hen. She sank back against the freshly fluffed pillow and waited as he finished straightening covers. Then he sat beside her on the bed and tenderly tucked a piece of hair behind her ear.

"Thank God I found you."

"Yes," she agreed. "Thank you."

He leaned forward and gave her a brief kiss. He smiled crookedly. "Oops. I shouldn't have done that."

She narrowed her eyes. "Why not?"

"'Cuz I should have done this."

His hot lips melted against hers, and she closed her eyes to revel in it. The warmth of his tongue hinted at the fire raging inside him. He broke for air, and she was amazed to find her cheek wet. She looked into his watery eyes.

"I was afraid," he admitted. "Twice in less than a week you have nearly sent me to my own grave. You have to stop doing that."

Her own eyes teared up as she pulled him into a hug. "Don't you know I have nine lives?"

He snorted. "Well, let's not test the other seven."

He pulled back while at the same time grabbing her hand. He slipped a sparkling diamond ring on her finger. "Now it's official. Please be my wife."

Her heart swelled up with love, and she answered him with a kiss. He smiled like a schoolboy. "Now *that* I guess I should've done."

Epilogue

Twelve Months Later

Emily sat in the parlor, holding a tiny baby girl. "So are you going to accept Luke's offer?"

"I think it would be best if Rachel and I go at it on our own. I'm thinking of moving to Texas," Brent stated. "Get a fresh start."

He touched her arm lightly. "What about you? Are you happy?"

She looked at the simple diamond ring on her left hand and warmth flooded through her heart. "Yep. I'm right where I'm supposed to be. I'm home."

The baby mewed, drawing their attention. Emily traced a finger over the soft cheek. She sighed. "I pray that everything works out with ours. Luke doesn't deserve any more pain."

"He told me that he intends on having the best doctor money can buy. Don't worry," Brent assured her.

She remained quiet for a second, then shook her head free of disturbing thoughts. *A mother-to-be should think positive,* she told herself.

"Little Sarah sure is beautiful," she whispered, unable to take her eyes off the baby.

"I know. Makes me glad I paid that fella to cut my arm."

Convicted of Love

Part 3:

Maggie

Chapter 1

March 27, 1891
Friday Evening
New Orleans, Social Gathering

The top of Maggie's hand stung. She had been reaching for a pastry when a frilly blue fan popped against her knuckles. She turned to the tall brunette beside her.

"I do believe you have had your limit, Margarite," stated her snooty cousin.

Of course, it's Penelope Pain, she thought rebelliously. Maggie had quickly grown tired of her new chaperone. Unfortunately, she was stuck with her, unless she wanted to spend the next eternity in her room.

Penelope smiled superficially and lowered her voice. "The past year you served as a convict won't compare to the time you're going to serve with me."

Maggie frowned and reached for a carrot instead. Her cousin smiled approvingly. "Once you're married, you can become fat as a pig if you like, but not now."

"Penelope, he's here."

She whirled around dramatically, searching the crowded room. She paid little attention to the news bearer, a pretty blonde with a pert little nose.

"Where?"

The blonde raised a dainty, glove-clad finger. "I saw him with his friends over there."

Without another word, Penelope hurried in the direction indicated. Maggie was left standing awkwardly with the blonde girl. She chewed on her lip as her heart jumped in her throat and cut off air.

"Hello, Darlene."

The blonde barely glanced at Maggie. She stuck her pert little nose higher in the air. "I don't socialize with convicts."

Maggie's eyes watered as she watched Darlene turn on her heel and walk away. Her spirits sank to her feet, and since Penelope wasn't near, she grabbed a small pastry and popped it in her mouth. She had hoped things wouldn't be this way, but deep in her heart, she knew society would always look down on her. For her mother's sake, however, she would try to fit in.

"Was that good?"

Maggie whirled around, preparing to defend her food choice. Her words stuck in her mouth as she stared up into warm, honey brown eyes. Her insides melted at his handsomeness, and she lost all comprehensive thought. Before she could even form a word, though, someone interrupted them.

"Why, look Darlene. If it isn't Miles Clinton Louis McAndrew," Penelope gushed from behind Maggie. "The third."

Embarrassment crossed his face at the long name. He smiled charmingly at Maggie, showing perfectly even teeth. "I prefer Clint."

Maggie grinned despite her inner awkwardness. She'd never been that great with men, and after the deception of her last boyfriend, Brent Lafourche, she didn't completely trust any of them. There was, however, something different about this one.

Penelope stepped between them. "How is your dear mother, Clinton? I heard she's been ill."

"She's fine, Penny. It was a mere cold." He looked past her at Maggie. "You haven't introduced me to your friend."

Penelope looked over her shoulder, acting as if she had just seen Maggie. "Oh, yes, this is my cousin, Margarite Marie Lafitte. She recently came home from serving one year in prison."

Maggie's heart stopped, and her cheeks flushed red. Her eyes watered as she ducked her head. She wanted to crawl under a table and die, but her feet wouldn't move.

"Is she attending classes at Newcomb College?" he inquired, ignoring Penelope's obvious spitefulness.

Timidly, Maggie chanced a peek at him. She wondered why he didn't ridicule her like her cousin's other friends had.

"Ha," Penelope snorted, snapping open her fan and waving it over her face. "That'll be the day."

A boy suddenly appeared at her elbow. "Would you like to dance, Penelope?"

She rolled her eyes in his direction. "No thank you, Reginald. I believe Clinton was about to ask."

"No I wasn't."

Pink flooded Penelope's face, but she quickly composed herself. She held out her hand. "Yes, Reginald. That would be lovely. Clinton is obviously tired from his weekend hunting trip."

"No I'm not."

Ignoring his remark, she practically pulled Reginald off his feet as she headed through the crowd of college students. Maggie crossed her arms and stared at the floor. She held back a smile at the thought of actually watching someone put her cousin in her place.

"Margarite."

Her head snapped up. "Maggie."

Clint grinned. "It's nice to see you don't uphold formalities like your cousin."

She shrugged. "She has good intentions."

"Yeah, to make herself look good," he sneered. "Anyway, would you like to dance?"

Maggie's eyes widened. "I, uh, I..."

He grabbed her hand and pulled her to the ballroom floor. "Great."

Chapter 2

March 28, 1891
Saturday
French Quarter

Maggie followed reluctantly behind Penelope, Darlene and Amy. She struggled to keep her spirits up, which always seemed to sink when she was around her cousin. She had looked forward to the shopping trip all week, but after carrying their purchases all morning, she was ready to return home. Besides, the comments her cousin had said when they entered the first store kept swirling in her head.

"Now, Margarite, please keep your fingers to yourself."

Her mouth had dropped as she had blurted, "I wasn't convicted of stealing."

"Oh, right, that was your friend, Candace."

"Camille," Maggie had corrected. "And she didn't steal anything. It was a big misunderstanding."

Penelope had merely rolled her eyes and turned her back on Maggie. "If that's what you think, dear cousin."

Maggie snapped back to the present as she walked into Darlene, who had stopped abruptly in the middle of the sidewalk. Dropping the cloth shopping bag, she grabbed the girl's arm before she ended up on her rear. Darlene, however, yanked her arm away and sneered.

"Gosh, Margarite, watch where you're going."

"Margarite," Penelope complained. She quickly picked up the shopping bag and pulled out a box. Seconds later, a glass swan twinkled in the sunlight, and Penelope breathed a sigh of relief. "If you had broken this…"

"I am so sorry, Penelope. I promise I'll be more careful," Maggie apologized.

"Yes, see that you do or you won't accompany me on the next trip."

"Penelope, it's the Court of Two Sisters," Amy said excitedly. "I heard they have a new shipment of fans straight from Paris, and they are exquisite."

The trio burst into conversation about the latest fashions as they entered the store. Maggie was left alone on the sidewalk. She picked up the bag and hesitated, thinking it would be so easy to slip away. Her mother's disapproving face flashed in her head, and she sighed. Looking at her feet, she reached for the doorknob, but another grabbed it first.

"Allow me."

Startled, she looked up into honey-brown eyes. She smiled as her day instantly brightened. "Well, hello, Miles Clinton Louis McAndrew."

He rolled his eyes. "You forgot the Third, Margarite Marie Lafitte."

She smiled wider. "What brings you to the Court of Two sisters? Looking for the latest ball gown?"

"Why, how did you know?" he gushed as femininely as possible. He batted his eyes to add more effect.

She giggled. "Oh, sir, I do believe your type is better served down around Bourbon Street."

His face grew serious. "And how would a dove such as yourself know of such things?"

Her smile faded as she thought of the escapades with Brent. "I...I'd rather not say, sir."

His hand cupped her face, instantly wanting to squash the pain that surfaced in her eyes. "I'm sorry. I didn't mean—"

A female standing behind him cleared her throat. "Must I wait all day for you to enter?"

Clint looked over his shoulder. "Maggie, this is Luci, my sister and my purpose for visiting the Court of Two Sisters."

"Hello, Maggie. It's a pleasure to meet you. Now, if you'll excuse me, I'd like to get inside before those three social brats take everything."

Maggie smiled and stepped aside to let the brunette in. "Of course."

Luci stood her ground and motioned with her hand. "After you, dear. You were here first."

"It's alright. I don't mind."

"Well, I do," Luci stated firmly.

"If one of you don't move, I'll gladly go first and gentlemanly attitude be damned," Clint growled in a friendly way.

Maggie smiled and quickly stepped inside. The second she crossed the doorway, however, Penelope pounced on her.

"Where have you been?" She whispered, taking her by the elbow. She thrust three parasols into Maggie's hand. "Hold these while we shop."

Maggie struggled with the parasols and the full shopping bag, trying to find an easy way to hold all of them. A masculine hand took the shopping bag from her, and she smiled gratefully up at Clint. Unfortunately, the action drew Penelope's attention to his presence. Her demeanor changed instantly.

"Why, Miles Clinton," she trilled. "What a pleasure it is to see you."

"Hello, Penny."

"What on earth are you doing?" she admonished as she attached herself to his arm. She pulled the shopping bag from his grasp. "Margarite, take this."

She practically threw the bag at Maggie and then proceeded to guide the shell-shocked man further into the store, chattering about how he just had to help her pick out a suitable gown for Friday's soirée. Maggie simply stared enviously at them.

"I shouldn't worry, dear."

Maggie turned to Luci, pretending ignorance. "About what?"

"He'll shake her soon."

Maggie narrowed her eyes. "How can you be so sure?"

Luci smiled secretively. "I know my brother, and she's not his type."

Maggie returned to staring at Clint and Penelope. "But, she's every man's type."

Luci grimaced. "I pity every man, then."

Maggie glanced queerly at her. "Why? She's quite a catch—beauty, grace, money. Even I can see someone would be crazy not to want her."

Luci leaned over the table. "I know she's your cousin, so excuse me for saying so, but the sun does not rise and set with Miss Penelope Lafitte."

Family loyalty rose to the surface, and despite the fact that she liked this young woman, Maggie felt obliged to defend her cousin. Sticking her nose high in the air, she replied, "Well, Miss McAndrew, I daresay this conversation is over. Good day to you."

Luci merely shrugged as Maggie sauntered past. "I was just expressing an opinion. Pardon me."

Chapter 3

Same Day
Courtyard of Court of Two Sisters

Maggie sat between Penelope and Darlene as they partook of tea and cakes. Fortunately, she had a good view of Clint, who sat on the other side of Penelope. However, she avoided eye contact with his sister, who was on his left and looked not at all pleased at sharing a table with the three brats of society.

Penelope slid her cup of tea in front of Maggie. "Two sugars and a touch of milk."

Without hesitation, Maggie obliged her cousin's request, but then she found herself preparing Darlene's as well as Amy's. All the while, she felt the disapproving stare of Luci, which she tried to ignore.

Just as she was about to fix her own tea, Penelope asked, "Would you be a doll, Margarite, and butter my scone?"

Maggie sighed as a weight pressed down on her soul. She felt as if she were still serving time. If she bucked the system, however, she'd be sent to a convent. She couldn't afford to aggravate Penelope, so she smothered the rebellion that rose in her chest and buttered the scone.

After she ate her own scone, she dared a glance at Clint

and found he was staring at her despite having his ear talked off by Penelope. She blushed and looked at her empty plate. She reached for another treat only to have her hand tapped with a fan.

"You've had your limit," Penelope smiled politely.

Feeling like a child, Maggie sat back, fighting the urge to pout. Her stomach rumbled despite the one scone she had eaten. "But, Penelope, I have had nothing to eat all day."

Her cousin glared at her. "You had breakfast."

"One egg and a piece of toast wouldn't hold a canary all day," Maggie grumbled.

"You may have more tea but no milk."

Luci jumped to her feet. "I've seen enough, Clint. I'm leaving, with or without you."

As his sister huffed away, Clint rose slowly to his feet. His eyes on Maggie, he asked, "May I call on you tomorrow?"

"Why, certainly," Penelope gushed, confident he was asking her.

He looked pointedly at Penelope. "I was asking Maggie."

Penelope caught herself before her mouth dropped open. Her eyes hooded, she turned to Maggie, waiting for the girl's response. When she just stared at him dumbfounded, Penelope kicked her under the table. Maggie jumped.

"Why, yes, that would be lovely."

"Two o'clock then?"

Maggie nodded. "Yes."

Clint hurried after his sister, and Maggie nervously avoided Penelope's eyes. The tension at the table increased until Amy chirped, "I thought Miles was courting you, Penelope. Why is he calling on Margarite?"

Darlene elbowed her, making her whine. Penelope merely smiled, but it didn't reach her eyes.

"That's fine. I see no problem with him calling on our little jailbird. It's apparent he prefers tainted goods. I'll have to ensure nothing fortuitous occurs, as her chaperone, of course."

Though right beside Penelope, Maggie heard not a word. She had a silly smile on her face as she contemplated Clint's interest in her. *Mother will be so pleased,* she thought happily.

* * * *

"Margarite, I cannot believe you would steal your cousin's beau," Mrs. Lafitte huffed.

"But, mother, he's never even called on her. Not once," Maggie protested.

"That is beside the point. I forbid it."

"Aunt Ellen." Penelope placed her hand on the older woman's arm. "Let him come. Once he's here, we can find some excuse to get Margarite out of the room."

Maggie pursed her lips as her eyes filled with tears. She felt like Cinderella, but what made it worse was that she wasn't a stepchild. It hurt that her own mother took her cousin's side and plotted against her.

"But I thought you wanted to see me married," she whispered.

"I do, Margarite, but not to your cousin's intended," she admonished.

"But he doesn't even like her," Maggie proclaimed loudly.

Her mother closed her eyes to keep from flying into a rage. Then she steeled her voice. "You will do as I say, Margarite, or I will ship you to a convent so fast..."

Maggie hung her head. "Yes, Mother."

Chapter 4

March 29, 1891
Sunday

Maggie tried to relax as she sat between Penelope and her mother on the settee. Clint sat in her father's wing-backed chair. He kept polite conversation, but she could tell by the look on his face that he was ready to escape. He must have realized that after fifteen minutes of chitchat, they were not going to have any time alone.

The maid finally entered with the tea, and Maggie held her breath. She expected Penelope to ask her to fix her tea, but thankfully she did not.

"So, Mr. McAndrew," her mother began. "Are you attending college?"

"Yes, ma'am, and please, call me Clint," he replied and took a gulp of tea.

"What are you studying?"

"Law."

Her mother raised an eyebrow. "Penelope is attending Newcomb College and is doing quite well."

"Yes, ma'am, so I've heard. Are you attending as well, Maggie?"

"Margarite is not suited for such things," her mother

stated.

"Why do you say that? From my perspective, she's quite intelligent," he stated firmly.

Maggie blushed and ducked her head. "Well, I was hoping to apply in the fall."

Penelope choked on her tea but kept her thoughts to herself, for once. Maggie glared at her briefly before looking at her mother. "I would like to learn more about cooking. While I was away, I spent a lot of time with the cook."

Her mother's eyes widened. "That's enough, Margarite. We'll discuss it later."

Maggie realized her faux pas and looked anxiously at Clint. He was about to speak but something changed his mind. Instead, he grabbed a small cake and popped it in his mouth. Unable to look away, Maggie found herself mesmerized by his lips, and only the feeling of warm liquid on her lap drew her eyes away from him. Her teacup had been knocked out of her hand as Penelope had reached for a pastry.

"Oh, how clumsy of me," her cousin cooed falsely.

"You should go change," her mother stated.

Maggie gulped, realizing this was the moment they had been calculating for. She hesitated, carefully weighing her reaction. One look at Clint gave her all the courage she needed.

"No, mother, I'm fine. 'Tis but a tad damp."

"Nonsense, Margarite. Go change."

Raising her chin, she looked calmly at her mother. "No."

"Margarite," Penelope whispered a touch angrily. "Don't make a scene."

Clint set his cup and saucer down and stood. "I think it's time I took my leave. I have some studying to do."

Penelope rose elegantly. "I shall see you to the door."

"Well, I was wondering if I might have a word with Maggie, if you don't mind, Mrs. Lafitte."

With her fingers crossed but out of sight, Maggie watched her mother purse her lips. A few seconds later, she nodded, carefully avoiding Penelope's eyes. "I suppose a moment or two on the front porch will be fine."

Maggie released the breath she had been holding and practically jumped to her feet. She headed for the front door, only to stop at Clint's next words.

"Mrs. Lafitte, forgive me if I overstep my bounds, but I feel it necessary to point out that educated men like educated women."

Maggie bit her lip and waited for her mother to explode. When not a sound was made, she turned to see her mother quietly assessing the young man before her. He never flinched but stared her surely in the eye.

"I feel Maggie's attendance at Newcomb would better prepare her for marriage," he boldly continued.

Her mother raised an eyebrow. "Mr. McAndrew, might I ask your intentions toward my daughter?"

Clint glanced briefly at Maggie before addressing the question. "My intentions are honorable, I assure you of that, Mrs. Lafitte."

The older lady slowly rose to her feet. "My daughter has been hurt quite grievously. I'll not have her drawn into any outrageous shenanigans. Do you understand, Mr. McAndrew?"

"Yes, ma'am. I give my word as a gentleman she shall not be hurt by me."

"A boy of your age promised me that very thing some years ago," her mother stated firmly. "He broke it."

Clint crossed his arms and tilted his head to the side. "If a man cannot abide by his words, then he should not utter them."

An awkward silence filled the room as everyone waited

for Mrs. Lafitte's response. She finally smiled as pleasantly as possible. "Well, we shall have to see about that, won't we?"

He dipped his head in acknowledgment. "Thank you for the tea and cakes, Mrs. Lafitte. It was very nice to meet you."

Then, ignoring Penelope, he hurried to Maggie and led her outside. Once alone, he took her hands in his and stared warmly at her. "You are so pretty."

She blushed and ducked her head, but he lifted her chin with his fingers. His warm brown eyes had her insides melting. She struggled with the urge to step closer to him.

"I want to kiss you," he whispered. "But I feel several pairs of eyes staring at us."

She smiled wistfully. "I don't think that would be appropriate, but if it were, I wouldn't mind at all."

"Perhaps next time, then," he said, licking his lips in anticipation. "Do you think you'll be at the party on Friday?"

"Not even Penelope could keep me away."

Chapter 5

April 3, 1891
Friday Afternoon

"Mother, you know she's not sick," Maggie stated. "She's just pretending. She doesn't want me going with her to the party this evening because she knows Clint will be there."

Mrs. Lafitte stopped sewing. "Margarite, please. She wouldn't do that."

She knelt at her mother's feet. "Please, mother. Please let me go without her. She's just being spiteful. Can't you see Clint has no interest in her?"

Her mother sighed. "I realize I was wrong about that. Penelope...well, the way she carried on about him."

Maggie sat back on her heels and stared at her hand with feigned interest. Then she breathed in deeply and said, "I'm nineteen, mother. I made a mistake. Haven't I paid for it already?"

Her mother's silence made her heart beat faster. *Please, please, please,* she thought, not daring to even look up.

"The return of my trust has to be earned, and I suppose I shall have to test you sooner or later."

Maggie's face brightened, and she threw her arms around her mother. Then she kissed her on the cheek and laughed.

Her mother smiled despite her misgivings.

"Why, Margarite, I've never seen you so excited. Not even when Brent first began to court you."

Maggie refused to let thoughts of him cloud her day. "I promise to be a good girl, mother. You shall not regret this."

* * * *

Maggie sat on a bench beside Clint, looking at the twinkling stars. They had snuck away from the stifling party and were in the gazebo, which was in the center of an immense garden. The house was an acre or so away, and so they felt they had some privacy.

The scent of gardenias tickled her nose. Tilting her head, she closed her eyes and breathed in deeply. Thus, she was completely unprepared for the soft kiss on her bare shoulder.

Her eyes flew open, and she saw that Clint's face was inches from hers. Unconsciously turning toward him, she held her breath in anticipation as he gently placed both hands on her face and lowered his head. His lips touched hers briefly, and when she didn't object, he kissed her again.

She drowned in the softness of his lips against hers, and when his kiss deepened, she loved the way he tasted like strawberries and cream. Eyes closed, she floated willingly on cloud nine, forgetting everything but him.

They kissed for several minutes, only pausing to take breaths of air. He was gentle with her, kissing her cheeks and eyes, making her feel as if she were the most beautiful girl in the world. He lingered on her neck, careful not to leave any red marks. Shivers coursed through her, and she leaned closer to him, wanting more, but not completely understanding what it was she craved.

He stopped kissing her and leaned his forehead against hers. His heart beat rapidly against the palm of her hand, and she watched his face curiously. "What's wrong?"

"I think we need to stop."

"But I want more," she whispered huskily.

He smiled crookedly. "So do I, but we must wait."

Disappointed, she closed her eyes and tried to get her own heart to slow down.

"My, my, what a charming display."

Startled, Maggie looked at the gazebo entrance. Penelope stood with one hand holding a lantern and the other on her hip. "Just wait until Aunt Ellen hears about this," she stated smugly.

Guiltily, Maggie and Clint jumped apart. "Penelope, no. Please don't tell mother."

As the brunette slowly climbed the gazebo steps, Clint stood defensively in front of Maggie, acting as a shield. "Nothing happened here. A few kisses, that's all."

She stopped in front of him and held the lantern high so as to see his face better. "Oh really, Mr. Keep My Promise? I thought your intentions were honorable, Clinton."

"They are."

"Sneaking out here doesn't look honorable to me."

Maggie's knees tremble uncontrollably. "Please, Penelope. I'll do anything you ask. Please don't tell mother."

The brunette paused thoughtfully. "Anything?"

"Yes, anything."

"What about you, Clinton? Are you willing to do anything to keep Mrs. Lafitte from finding out you were ravaging her daughter?"

He hesitated suspiciously. He glanced back at Maggie, and as the lantern's flame danced over the fear in her eyes, he reluctantly looked back at Penelope. Guardedly, he replied, "Yes, anything."

A devilish smile played on her face. She waited several second before speaking. "Then court me instead of her, and I won't say a word."

Maggie's heart lurched. "No."

"That's blackmail," Clint growled.

"Prove it."

He crossed his arms. "Prove that we were kissing."

She laughed wickedly. "Oh, darling, I don't have to prove that. It's my word over hers, and I think in light of her past, guess who dear Mama will believe?"

He gritted his teeth, trying to decide what to do. He turned to Maggie and hated the sight of pain and fear on her face. He knelt before her.

"What do you want me to do?" he whispered, searching her eyes that glowed in the lantern's flame.

She nibbled on her fingernail with eyes wide. Maggie refused to look at Penelope. She also refused to cry. If she spoke, she would. So she shrugged her shoulders, hating the way her stomach twisted.

"I won't come between you and your mother," he said. "There's too much strain on your relationship as it is."

She finally found her voice. "But I really, really like you."

His frown softened, and he cupped her cheek. "And I you."

"Oh, this is so touching," Penelope snarled. She snapped her fingers. "Time's a spinning. Yea or nay, Clinton?"

Making his decision, he slowly stood and faced her. "You breath a word to Mrs. Lafitte, and it's off, Penelope. Do you understand me?"

Chapter 6

Maggie's eyes felt red and puffy, and her nose felt like someone had stuffed it with handkerchiefs. It was sore to touch, and she told herself that she had to stop crying. Clint was not the last man on earth. At least, that's what her head kept saying. Her heart, on the other hand, strongly disagreed.

The bedroom door flew open and hit the wall with a bang. She jumped, but when she saw who it was, she pulled the covers over her head.

"Go away, Penelope."

The blanket was ripped away, revealing that she was still in her nightgown. Her cousin rolled her eyes and snorted in disgust. She folded her arms over her bosom and glared at Maggie.

"Please tell me you're not still pining away for Clint."

Tears sprang to Maggie's eyes, and she blinked them away. "I'm just not feeling well. Leave me alone."

"Liar. Get over it, Margarite. I'm not giving him back."

She leaned down and yanked Maggie's ear. "If you ruin this for me, I swear you'll regret it."

Before she could stop herself, Maggie slapped Penelope's cheek. Shock registered on both their faces, and Maggie quickly scrambled to the other side of the bed. Her bare feet wiggled against the hard wood floor.

"I'm sorry," she said anxiously.

Penelope pulled her shoulders back and stuck her head up high. Maggie's fingers had left a slight red mark. Her eyes glittered maliciously. "Since you're not feeling well, maybe you should stay home from the party tonight. Clint and I need some time alone anyway."

Maggie hurried to correct the situation. "No, no, I'm fine."

She rushed to her closet and pulled out her gown. She held it to her chest and faced Penelope. "See? It won't take me long to get ready."

Penelope glared at her and pursed her lips. "I have to freshen up. Meet me downstairs in one hour."

* * * *

As she paced the foyer, Maggie tapped her fan against her gloved hand impatiently. Penelope was late, but she was anxious to see Clint. She hoped he would arrive before her cousin came down. She was determined to steal all the time she could with him.

Their butler entered the hall and looked at her curiously. "Are you feeling better, Miss Maggie?"

Perplexed, she smiled. "Yes, sir. I'm just waiting for Penelope."

He tilted his head. "Miss Penelope left with Master Clinton a half hour ago. She said you were ill and had chosen to stay home."

Maggie's mouth fell open. The wretched girl had left her at home on purpose. She narrowed her eyes and chewed her lip. "I am quite well now. Would you please have the carriage brought around for me?"

* * * *

Maggie tapped Penelope on the shoulder. "I brought you some punch."

She resisted the urge to throw it on her. However, she noted with great satisfaction the annoyance on her cousin's face. It made her glad she had been brave enough to show up on her own.

"Maggie, you should be in bed. You might be contagious."

The group took a step away from Maggie as if she had the plague, all except Clint. He took great concern over her supposed illness. He placed a hand on her forehead.

"You don't have a fever, although your face is a tad puffy. What happened?"

She blushed and ducked her head. "I got bit by a plecia nearctica."

Clint crinkled his face as he contemplated her answer. *Love bugs don't bite.*

He took her hand in his absentmindedly. She froze, aware that everyone was watching. She was reluctant to pull her hand free as his felt so good and warm and secure. The group became silent, and Clint started rubbing her hand with both of his. She knew then that he had realized her mistake and was attempting to cover it up.

"Your hands are freezing."

He then let go of her and reluctantly grabbed Penelope's hand. His eyes were mixed with sorrow and anger, and Maggie's heart throbbed painfully. She bit her lip to stave the tears.

An awkward silence fell upon them, and she wished she hadn't come. She wished she hadn't been bold and wondered why she had been. It wasn't in her nature to take things into her own hands. She recalled how she had slapped Penelope earlier, and while she tried to feel remorseful, she ended up smiling secretively instead.

"Let's dance, darling."

Penelope pulled Clint away, and the other two couples followed. Maggie was left to stand alone. Clint looked woefully back at her, and she suddenly felt bad for him. After all, he was the one who had to dance with a witch.

She sighed, crossed her arms, and took her place beside the other wallflowers. She watched longingly as Clint whirled Penelope around the dance floor. She tried to focus on others in the crowd, but the two kept popping into view. Disheartened, she fled the ballroom, opting for fresh air to clear her troubled mind.

* * * *

Maggie dashed into the closest room. Penelope had been hounding her the entire evening. She had to fetch her this or fetch her that, and Maggie knew exactly how Cinderella felt. So she had escaped at the first opportunity she could get. She leaned her cheek against the wood door and spread her fingers over its grains. It smelled of fresh lemon oil, and she wished she could find a love that was as solid as the oak.

"Should I leave you and the door alone?"

Startled, she whirled around to find Clint sitting behind the desk with his feet propped up. He puffed on a fat cigar and blew smoke rings in the air.

"What are you doing?" she whispered nervously.

"Partaking of a lovely after-dinner tradition."

She double-checked the room to ensure they were alone. "But they aren't yours."

He patted his breast pocket. "Of course they are. I brought them from home."

She relaxed and leaned against the door. "Oh. Good."

He held out his cigar. "Come and try it."

She shook her head and wrinkled her nose. "No, ladies don't do that."

"I'm not suggesting you make a habit of it."

She eyed him warily and shook her head again. "No."

Satisfied, he nodded in agreement. "Good. Now, why can't you be that way with your cousin?"

She groaned and leaned her head back against the door. Maggie listened to the creaking his chair made as he rocked. She knew he was right, but her cousin intimidated her. She knew she had to change but was having a hard time doing it.

Clint suddenly appeared in front of her. His big, warm hands settled on her waist. She found the musky scent of his cologne pleasing, and her senses began to swirl. She felt as if she were caught in a sweet fog. His head dipped down, and his lips fondled her own.

Maggie couldn't believe he was kissing her. Her arms slipped around his neck, and her fingers played with his silky hair. She wondered if she was dreaming and didn't want to wake if she were.

His hot lips sucked on her lower lip until it was swollen and puffy. He kissed her chin and then followed her jaw line to her neck. His teeth nibbled her soft earlobe, and she shivered with unexplained need. He cupped her face, and she saw a seriousness in his eyes that scared her. His voice was thick and gruff.

"There. *Now* you've been bitten by a love bug."

She smiled. "We better get back. She'll be—"

He cut her off with more kisses. He wrapped her hair around his fingers and rubbed it against his cheek. She couldn't quit staring into his eyes. If the door hadn't held her up, she'd have crumbled to the floor.

Then she heard Penelope calling Clint's name. He stepped back, and her face and neck burned at the thought of what they had been doing. If Penelope found out, there would be hell to pay. Casually, he pulled out his cigar, stuck it between his teeth and re-lit it.

"I'll see you tomorrow at the picnic," he whispered and left her alone in the library.

She listened at the door as he led Penelope away. Then she sighed, thinking of the way he had looked at her. He didn't sneer in contempt or boss her like she was a servant. Maggie knew he wanted her but couldn't figure out why. She did know that she liked him, and no matter what happened, she always would.

Chapter 7

Maggie woke to the sound of someone screaming. She jumped out of bed and hurried to Penelope's room. Her mother stood behind her cousin as she sat at her vanity.

"What's wrong?" she asked.

When she made eye contact with her mother, she tried not to laugh as the older lady rolled her eyes. "Your cousin has a blemish."

Her mother stepped aside, and Maggie stared at Penelope's reflection in the mirror. In the middle of her forehead was a rather large red bump.

"Oh, Penny," she gushed. "I hope it doesn't leave a pock mark."

"Hush up, Maggie," Penelope snarled.

Her mother tapped her cousin's shoulder. "That'll be enough."

"I'm ruined, Aunt Ellen," Penelope moaned. She crossed her arms and pouted.

A glimmer of hope entered Maggie's heart. As nonchalantly as possible, she said, "So I guess you won't be going to the picnic then."

Penelope turned in her chair and stared coldly at her. "Oh, I'm going. Rest assured."

Maggie's shoulders drooped as the shadow fell back over

her heart. She turned on her heel and headed back to her own room. Something stopped her in mid-stride, however, and it felt like a volcano was erupting in her. Ever so slowly, she turned to face Penelope.

"Well, maybe Clint won't notice it. After all, it's really me he likes," she said challengingly before leaving the room. She half expected her cousin to push her from behind and was mildly shocked when she made it to her room unscathed.

* * * *

Maggie sat on a blanket spread out in front of a lake. They were at Darlene's country getaway, and she knew her invitation had only been because of Penelope. She and Darlene were definitely not friends.

Three white ducks glided across the calm lake, making ripples across its smooth surface. One suddenly took off after the other, and they flew madly across the lake. It reminded her of Penelope chasing Clint.

"Speak of the devil," she mumbled as the two strolled up. Penelope hung all over Clint, and her big, floppy hat continuously hit his head. He looked aggravated, but, as usual, Penelope was oblivious to it.

"Are you hungry, Clint?" Maggie asked as she pulled out food from the picnic basket.

"Famished." He knelt and began to help her. "What do we have?"

"Sandwiches, fruit, pastries."

"You only get one, Maggie," Penelope piped in. "No man likes a heavyset wife."

Clint grunted. "Oh, I don't know about that. I like a bit of flesh on my women. Besides, my father loves my mother deeply, and she's no dainty doll."

Maggie couldn't help but smile at Penelope's shocked expression. She hid it, though. Her newfound boldness did have its limits. She took her wide-brimmed hat off and shook out her hair. A breeze chose that moment to sift over them, and she closed her eyes to enjoy its touch. When she opened them, Clint was staring at her with a hungry look. She knew it had nothing to do with food. She remembered his kisses from the night before and blushed. Thankfully, her cousin didn't notice.

"So, Mags, have you decided about college yet?" Clint asked before taking a bite of his sandwich.

Penelope choked. "College? Margarite, you need to find a decent husband and not worry about nonsense. Convicts don't go to college."

Maggie's heart constricted at the word *convicts*. Clint, on the other hand, flew off the handle before she could even speak up.

"Damn it, Penny. Why must you continuously remind her of that? Can't you be nice for once in your life?"

Unruffled, she merely lifted her eyebrow. "Really, Clinton, must we make a scene?"

"I'll make a scene whenever I damn well please," he yelled at the top of his voice. "Why? Does it embarrass you?"

He leaned close to her but continued to talk loud. "Why don't you take off your hat, Penny? You've been holding on to it like it was a life preserver."

Swift as a cat, he pulled it off her head. Then he jumped to his feet and held it out of her reach. She cried in protest and beat on his chest with her little fists.

"Give it back," she wailed shrilly.

"What's the matter, Penny? 'Fraid someone will see that big bump on your forehead?" he whispered unmercifully.

Her eyes grew wide, and she took a step back. She covered her forehead with her hand as her eyes glittered dangerously. "You're being unusually mean today, Miles Clinton.

What has gotten into you?"

His jaw twitched in agitation as he stewed on her answer. Then he threw her hat at her feet and stormed off. Penelope grabbed it and started to go after him, but he turned and pointed a finger at her.

"Don't," he ordered.

Good sense finally got hold of her. She stopped, looked uncertainly at Maggie, and then huffed her way to where Darlene and her beau were sitting. Maggie sat still, uncertain of what to do. She watched Clint storm his way to the other side of the lake. She wanted to join him but knew Penelope wouldn't like it and would give her hell later.

After cleaning up the lunch mess, Maggie looked to see what her cousin was doing. As luck would have it, Penelope's little flock had moved closer to the house and were playing croquet. She was surprised Penelope hadn't forced her to join. The brat hardly ever let her out of sight when Clint was around.

Pretending fascination with the lake, Maggie casually strolled around it to where Clint was throwing rocks. He didn't stop but seemed to be venting his anger on the water.

"Hi."

"Hey," he grunted.

"Are you mad at me?"

He finally stopped and looked at her. "Yes and no."

"Oh."

"You have to be the one to stand up to her, Mags."

She watched the group that was now on the other side of the lake. They were still in their game, and she hoped they'd play the rest of the afternoon. She backed up to where she was hidden from their view by a group of trees. Then she crooked her finger and motioned for him to draw near.

His face still held the fury of a storm. Maggie tilted her

head and smiled. "Come here."

She stood on her tiptoes, wrapped her arms around his neck, and boldly pulled him into a kiss. It wasn't long or spectacular, but it was enough to get his attention. He growled softly and pinned her against the tree behind them.

"That's nice," he whispered against her mouth. "But I'm not the one you need to do that to."

She looked at him in shock. "What? I'm not kissing Penelope."

He laughed. "No, silly, you need to be bold with her and stand up for yourself."

She distracted him by planting kisses all over his face. He succumbed to her gentle persuasion and took charge of the situation. He gave her a proper and thorough kiss. Their interlude was short-lived. Maggie cringed at the sound of Penelope's voice.

"Clint? Where are you?"

He motioned for Maggie to stay put, and he left to answer the call of the shrew. She waited for what seemed like forever before cautiously peering around the tree. She hoped they had moved far away so she could make her escape.

They hadn't moved an inch. In fact, they were in a heated discussion. Penelope had her back to Maggie, however, and she watched Clint's face as he argued. He looked briefly at her before pulling her cousin into his arms. Then, with his eyes firmly on Maggie, he kissed the wench.

Maggie's hand flew to her mouth, and her heart shattered. The wounded mouse came back, and she ducked behind the tree, hoping to avoid him for the rest of the picnic.

How could he do that?

"Hey, Maggie, are you playing hide-n-seek?"

Startled, she looked to her right and saw Amy. At least it wasn't Darlene. She and Amy actually got along, especially when Penelope wasn't around. She swiped a tear away.

"Uh, no," she stammered.

"That's a good idea."

Maggie looked to her left to find her cousin standing three feet away. Clint had his arm around her waist, but he gazed intently on Maggie. It was as if he were trying to tell her something. Hurting, she broke eye contact and focused on her cousin.

"What's a good idea?"

"Hide and seek."

* * * *

Maggie hid behind the tree where she had boldly kissed Clint earlier. She pressed her forehead to it, wishing she could go home. She surely did not feel like playing games, especially since Clint was now the seeker. Her intuition told her he would come after her, and a peek around the tree confirmed it. He was almost around the lake.

As she did not want to talk to him, she quickly and silently turned and ran into the woods. She chose another tree and knelt down. Peering around it, her eyes widened at the sight of Clint bearing down upon her. She squealed and took off running.

He was quicker, and he grabbed her around the waist and tried to stop her. Unfortunately, they ended up falling down. She was stunned for but a moment. Then she tried to scramble out from under. He pinned her down.

"Stop," he growled. "I wanna talk to you."

"Well," she panted. "I certainly don't want to talk to you."

He rolled her over on her back and held her hands above her head. Twigs and leaves were stuck in her hair, and she had a scratch on her cheek. Her face and neck were flushed becomingly, and he couldn't resist kissing her. She fought him, but her bucking only aroused him further. He ceased kissing her.

"Ugh," she spat. "Let me go. You can't have us both, if that's your plan. I'm not that much of a mouse."

"I don't want her."

"You kissed her."

"I had to keep her from finding you," he snarled. "She almost did, and then she would have figured it out. She's mean, not stupid."

She bit her lip, wondering if he were lying.

"I only tolerate her to get to you," he whispered. His eyes pleaded for her to understand. "I'll do whatever it takes to get you, even if it means duping the entire world."

Chapter 8

Maggie settled grumpily into the carriage. She had a cold and did not feel like going to snooty Darlene's birthday party. What made her feel worse was watching Penelope snuggle up to Clint. She sniffled and looked out of the window, feeling sorry for herself.

"I certainly hope you don't give me your cold," Penelope complained.

"I told you that I didn't want to come in the first place," Maggie grumbled.

"You've been cooped up all week. Fresh air will do you good. Besides, you need to go to all the parties. We have to find you a suitable husband before Aunt Ellen has a fit."

Maggie briefly met Clint's eyes, and her heart ached. Frowning, she looked back out the window as tears sprang to her eyes. She thought back to the day after their first kiss, when she had been forced to tell her mother that she had changed her mind about Clint. She never knew she could act so well

Perhaps I should run away to the theater, she thought grouchily.

"How long must we keep this ruse?" Clint asked irritably. "Haven't we been to enough events?"

Penelope pouted prettily. "I thought you loved me."

Maggie watched his flabbergasted face as he stared at her cousin. Then he asked, "Why do you want to be with someone who obviously can't stand you?"

Coldly, Penelope glared at him. "My parents are dead. Do you think I want to live with Aunt Ellen for the rest of my life?"

He held up his hand. "Whoa. Wait a minute. Where do you think this is going?"

"Marriages of convenience are quite common," she stated matter-of-factly.

"I'm not marrying you."

"Okay," she sang and pulled absentmindedly on her gloves. "I sure hope Aunt Ellen sends Margarite to St. Clare's Monastery, but I imagine she'll want to get her as far away from you as possible."

Clint crossed his arms and narrowed his eyes. "There are plenty who would gladly take you as a wife. God help them. Why are you so focused on me?"

She rolled her eyes. "Those boys are so boring. You, on the other hand…"

They settled into an uncomfortable silence. Maggie knew of Penelope's plans, had known since the day after the picnic. Since Penelope never left them alone, however, she'd had no chance whatsoever to warn him.

She peeked at him and was surprised to find him staring at her. He was angry. She could tell by the look in his eyes, and she wanted to hide from the storm that was about to break inside the carriage.

"Oh, look. Here we are," Penelope said as the carriage rolled to a stop.

Without waiting for his assistance, she quickly exited. Maggie knew Penelope was anxious to tell Darlene that Clint had proposed to her, for her cousin had confided just that morning that she would do whatever it took to become Mrs. Miles Clinton Louis McAndrew, III, even if it took setting steps in motion herself.

* * * *

"Would you care for some punch?"

Maggie jumped as the words were practically whispered in her ear. She turned to find Winston Hampshire standing quite close. She took several steps back and waved her fan in her face.

"You startled me."

"My apologies. How about that punch?"

She glanced at the dance floor. Penelope clung to Clint as they danced with the other couples. "That would be nice."

"Wait right here."

Moments later, he placed a cup in her hand. She smiled weakly. "Thank you, Mr. Hampshire."

"You're quite welcome, my dear."

When it became apparent he wasn't going to leave, she looked curiously at him. Most avoided her as if she had the plague, and since he was new to New Orleans, she assumed he knew nothing of her past.

"So you're from New York?"

"Yes. I found it rather cold, and when a business opportunity in this area arose, I gladly took advantage of it."

They slipped into awkward silence, and she found herself searching the dancing couples. When she couldn't find Clint and Penelope, she began to move away to search for them, but Winston placed his hand on her arm.

"Would you like to dance?"

Startled, she merely looked at him as if he were crazy. She couldn't fathom why the thirty-year-old man was so interested in her. He was handsome enough to have any woman he wanted. Then, remembering her manners, she politely declined. "I...I'm not feeling well. If you'll excuse me, I--"

"Allow me to fetch you a bite to eat, then."

She chewed on her lower lip, unsure of how to respond. Although nice enough, there was something about him she didn't like. She couldn't figure out what it was, though.

"Oh, that's quite all right. I'm fine."

"I insist."

And so she was reluctantly pulled into spending time with a man she hardly knew.

Chapter 9

Maggie sat on the front porch with a cup of coffee. She swallowed the last of it and set the cup on the small table next to her. A tiny, black paw reached up and gently tapped her leg. She looked into the face of her black and white cat. She smiled and scratched behind furry ears. Purring, the feline jumped into her lap and curled into a ball.

"Jasper, it's time to wake up not go to sleep," she softly admonished.

The cat's fur was silky as she rubbed her hand over him. Her thoughts turned to Winston Hampshire and his sudden interest in her. He had not left her side the previous night, to her annoyance. He was a nice man, but her heart belonged to someone else. She wanted to tell him so, but she didn't want to seem rude.

"Good morning, Miss Lafitte."

The object of her thoughts stood on the porch steps. She tried not to appear startled and forced herself to show her manners. "Mr. Hampshire, how nice to see you."

He was dressed in white from his head to his toe. He took his hat off and gave her a slight bow. He fiddled with the brim awkwardly. "I came to see if I might accompany you to church."

She didn't know what to say. "I, uh, well, that is, I suppose so…if father agrees."

Penelope chose that moment to step out of the house. She feigned surprise that Maggie distrusted. Her fan snapped open, and she waved it in front of her face.

"Why, Mr. Hampshire. What a delightful surprise."

He nodded his head in her direction. "Same here, Miss Penelope."

"What brings you to our humble home?" she asked.

The porch door interrupted his answer, and Maggie's parents appeared. Penelope practically gushed with enthusiasm.

"Look who's come to call on Margarite."

Maggie's eyes narrowed as it occurred to her that Mr. Hampshire had never given an answer. She began to suspect that someone else was behind his appearance. Penelope must have seen them conversing last night and taken it upon herself to encourage the man. Maggie was fuming by the time they left for church. Her manners were the only thing that kept her from blowing up. Although, Clint would probably have urged her to do just that.

* * * *

To Maggie's dismay, her mother invited Mr. Hampshire to lunch after church. She had fumed throughout the service and had intended to let loose on Penelope afterwards. His attendance at lunch, however, put a damper on her plans. So she vented her frustration in more subtle ways.

"Margarite, would you mind serving the tea?" Penelope chimed pleasantly.

Biting her cheek, she did as she was asked and added four cubes instead of two to her cousin's. She also added a few squirts of lemon, which the chit was allergic to. Penelope was too busy talking to notice. Several sips later, she dropped the cup and saucer in horror.

"Margarite, this has lemon in it."

"Oh, dear," she cooed. "You must have gotten mine by mistake."

"Aunt Ellen, is my face—"

Her mother patted her cousin's hand reassuringly. "You're fine. Mr. Hampshire, my niece is allergic to lemons."

He nodded understandingly. "If you don't mind my saying so, but I should think they not be allowed in the house then."

"But I love lemons," Maggie protested.

"But I'm sure you love your cousin more," he insisted.

She thought that there were many things she felt for her cousin, love being the least, but the laugh that choked her throat evaporated. His dark eyes seemed to convey a warning, and she shivered slightly under its intensity. A hand reached over her shoulder as the maid took the lemons away. She glanced at Penelope and was surprised that her cousin wasn't gloating.

"So, Mr. Hampshire, what brings you to New Orleans?" her father asked.

"I'm taking an extended holiday."

"And might I ask what type of business you do?" her father probed.

"My family is in shipping."

Mr. Lafitte nodded. "Ah, family money."

Maggie tried to pay attention as the men began talking business. She found her mind wandering, and as lunch was over, she cleared her throat.

"May I be excused?"

Her mother looked at her as if she had lost her mind. "Why, whatever for, dear?"

Maggie smiled weakly. "I feel a headache coming on."

Mr. Hampshire stood. "It's alright. I really must be on

my way. I hadn't realized the time. Thank you, Mrs. Lafitte, for such a lovely lunch."

"You are quite welcome," her mother smiled.

"I was wondering if I might be allowed to escort Miss Margarite to the opera on Friday night?"

Panic seized her as she looked frantically at her father. *Tell him no, please tell him no.*

Her father took no notice of her look. "Yes, yes, I think that would be a good idea. Penelope, why don't you and young Clint accompany them?"

Unusually silent, her cousin merely nodded. Maggie smiled. *The lemon must be taking effect. Lets hope it keeps her out of my hair for the rest of the afternoon.*

The men shook hands, and when Mr. Hampshire approached her, a devilish plan formed in her head. As he kissed the back of her hand, she smirked.

"Did you know I was convicted of a crime, Mr. Hampshire?"

Her mother gasped, and her father gruffed out her name. Her suitor, however, calmly stared her in the eyes.

"Why, yes, my dear. I know all about you," his eyes were cold as ice.."And rest assured, I have no qualms about it. I feel that you were with the wrong people at the wrong time."

Her plan having failed, she felt her cheeks flame. She knew people gossiped about her, but it hadn't hit home until now. Her chest constricted painfully. Her newfound courtier rubbed her hand fondly.

"The right company has found you now."

I doubt that, she thought grumpily. Her instincts warned her, and she was determined to listen. She hadn't before, and it had cost her dearly. Somehow, she'd convince her family that Mr. Right was Mr. Wrong.

* * * *

The following afternoon, Maggie was interrupted while playing the piano. The butler brought in an enormous floral arrangement consisting of sweet peas, periwinkles, bachelor's buttons, and pink carnations. The card stated, *History shall not repeat itself with me—Winston.*

Maggie rolled her eyes and tossed the card onto the floor. She picked the vase off the piano and handed it back to the butler.

"Put these in the carriage house please. I'm sure the horses will love the way they taste."

Before he could do as she asked, there was a loud knock on the front door. He answered it and came back with a pretty basket full of chocolates.

"It seems you have another admirer, Miss Margarite."

Her brows furrowed as she read the card. *Indulge to your hearts content—Your Secret Admirer.*

It only took a second for her to realize who it was from. Her cousin chose that moment to sashay in, and she hid the card in her hand. She didn't want anyone to know she had a 'secret admirer'.

"Well," Penelope drawled. "Are both of these for you?"

Maggie nodded as her flowers and sweets were inspected. She wished there were lemon flowers to chase her cousin away but would settle for lemon drops instead. She shook away her mischievous thoughts.

"Who are they from?"

"Winston."

The word was forced, and her cousin noticed. With a hand on her hip, she began the usual lecture. "Don't chase him away, Margarite. He's the only one willing to overlook your past discrepancies."

Maggie narrowed her eyes and whispered, "No, he's not."

Penelope ignored the remark. "Has Aunt Ellen seen these? She'll be so delighted."

Maggie snatched the basket of candy out of Penelope's hand. "These are mine."

"Well, pardon me," Penelope snapped. "I'm just looking out for your best interests."

"I can handle my interests just fine. Thank you very much."

Mrs. Lafitte appeared in the doorway. "Girls, I can hear you all over the house. What is going on?"

Seeing the gifts, she smiled as she smelled the flowers. "Are these from who I think?"

"Yes, Mama," Maggie answered. "I already gave instructions to feed them to the horses."

Her mother's eyes widened in shock. "You'll do no such thing."

"I don't want to lead him on. I have no interest in him."

Her mother stared sternly at her. "If he ends up asking for your hand, you had better accept it. Your ruined reputation has kept all the good catches away. Be thankful he's even interested."

Maggie's eyes watered. "When did you become so mean?"

Her mother's eyes swirled with emotions. "When my daughter disgraced me. Now, I suggest you display the flowers prominently on your dresser and be prompt in writing him a thank you note."

Chapter 10

Maggie tapped the end of the pen against her nose. She stared at her mother's handwriting and frowned. After ten attempts, it had come to this. She smiled at the simplicity of her first draft—'*Thank you*', which her mother had promptly crumpled and tossed across the room.

Sighing, she commenced to copying her mother's words. '*Mr. Hampshire, thank you for the lovely gifts. The flowers are exquisite, and the candy is as sweet as your thoughts. I look forward to Friday. Truly, Margarite.*'

She paused before writing about the candy. On one hand, it amused her to think of his confusion when he read about it. On the other hand, she thought it might be a good idea to let her mother know about her secret admirer. That would squelch any hasty decisions regarding Winston Hampshire. Her mind set, she found her mother on the back porch.

"Are you finished?"

Trying not to tremble, Maggie held out the secret admirer's card. "Hampshire did not send the candy. I don't know who did."

Mrs. Lafitte's brows drew together as she read the card. The silence was deafening as she watched her mother decide what to do. With pursed lips, her mother handed the card back to her.

"Omit the line and give the candy to charity."

Maggie's eyes widened, and her jaw dropped. Then she narrowed her eyes and clenched her teeth. "No. They're mine."

Mrs. Lafitte sighed in exasperation "Oh, for the love of God, Margarite, why can't you for once just do as you are told?"

Her three-year-old brother had been asleep in her mother's arms, but the harsh words woke him. He took his mother's attention for a few seconds, allowing Maggie to gather her thoughts. Somehow, she had to get through to the woman.

"And what if you had disregarded your secret admirer's gifts? Would I stand here before you today, Mama? Would little Paul?"

Shock flitted across the older woman's eyes. "I forgot I had told you that."

"Well, father still sends you secret admirer gifts," she whispered.

The matron's voice held less harshness in her reply. "Well, that's another matter entirely, dear."

Maggie stared her down, refusing to let her mother win this one. "How?"

Her mother took a moment's thought before replying. "I knew who my admirer was."

Maggie's cheeks reddened, and her eyes shifted guiltily away from her mother. She knew her mother was watching her intently and felt that the woman somehow knew that she was aware of her admirer as well. She was surprised at her mother's words.

"Keep the candy but omit the line."

Maggie smiled sheepishly and handed her the thank you card. "I already took the liberty."

Her mother passed no comment. She simply read it and handed it back. "Have it delivered immediately."

* * * *

Maggie stood with Clint outside the French Opera House on the corner of Bourbon and Toulouse Street. It was intermission, and she was fearful of falling asleep. She hated opera. Yet there she was in all her finery, waiting for Mr. Hampshire to bring her some refreshment. Penelope was inside, lost in conversation with one of her flighty friends. She was surprised that Clint had been allowed to escape.

She handed him a silver wrapped piece of chocolate. "Thank you."

He smiled secretively and popped the sweet into his mouth. "My pleasure."

"Are you as bored as I am?"

He nodded. "I'd give anything to be listening to some good ole ragtime."

Maggie's face brightened. "Oh, me, too!"

She leaned close to him in a conspiratorial manner. "Let's sneak away."

He hesitated while contemplating her offer. Then he offered his arm, and they slipped off into the night.

* * * *

Clint sat beside Maggie and slipped his hand in hers. He had decided a short trip on a horse-drawn streetcar would be more appropriate than taking her to some dingy club of disrepute. The various kinds of music on Bourbon Street would drift through the car's windows. Plus, they'd be able to talk.

"I think we'll have time to go to Canal Street and back."

She nodded. She seemed unable to take her eyes off him. He had cast a spell over her, and she feared if she looked away, he'd vanish forever. She reached up and brushed his bangs out of his eyes.

"You need a cut," she murmured.

He shrugged. "I like it long."

She tilted her head and twisted her lips. Then, making up her mind, she ruffled his hair. "There, that looks more like you. Please, no more pomade. It makes you look like a stuffed shirt."

He puffed out his chest and thrust out his chin. Then he pushed his lower lip out and lost his southern accent for a northern clip. "I dare say I disagree, Margarite. I would say I look smashing."

She batted her eyes and gave a false laugh. "Why, Mr. McAndrew, you are the conceited one. Remind me to have my slave girl slap you."

The smile faded from his face as he searched her eyes. "Is that how you see yourself?"

Her own mirth slipped away. "Don't."

"Don't what?"

"Can't we just forget about them and have some fun?" she pleaded.

He thought for a second before replying. "Ok, it's agreed. No more references to our so-called intendeds."

Her face paled. "I am not marrying him."

"I said so-called," he growled softly. "Somehow, I am going to find a way to make you mine."

He sealed his pledge with a kiss. She sank into him, instantly realizing how much she missed his lips. When they parted, she smiled dreamily. "A chocolate kiss."

His thumb rubbed her jaw line. "You'll find my heart is just as rich and sweet."

He stole a few more kisses. Then he rested his cheek against hers. She inhaled the refreshing scent of his cologne and sighed in content. The announcement of their street shattered their glass house. Reluctantly, they exited the streetcar and rushed to board the one returning to the opera house. They kissed the entire ride back.

* * * *

Maggie's heart lodged in her throat at the sight of the crowd pouring out of the opera house. Clint squeezed her hand reassuringly. They waited on the sidewalk for Penelope and Winston. To her relief, the two were deep in conversation as they walked out, and Clint had to grab Penelope's arm just to get her attention.

"Clint," she gushed as her cheeks flamed red. She glanced at Winston like a guilty lover, then attached herself to Clint's arm as if they'd never been apart. "The ending was just divine, wouldn't you agree?"

He gave her an odd look before slowly replying. "Yes."

"Winston is an avid opera fan. He attends every week," she stated proudly as they all walked toward their waiting carriage.

Inwardly, Maggie groaned and wondered if she were to be subjugated to opera every week. She prayed for God to save her from what appeared to be her destiny. She did not like Winston. Maggie had a bad feeling about him, but had no idea how to save herself. She glanced longingly at Clint and hoped he would come through with his promise to have her.

All the way home, she listened to Penelope prattle, and in the middle of the ride, it suddenly occurred to her that neither Winston nor Penelope had noticed that she and Clint had not returned to their seats. The realization had her looking at Clint in astonishment. His knowing smile lifted her spirits, and she smiled. Maybe future nights at the opera wouldn't be quite so bad, especially if the second half was spent like tonight.

Chapter 11

June 24, 1891
Wednesday

The smells from Café du Monde had lured Maggie to gaze in the restaurant longingly. It was very early, and her mother had sent her to the market to get some fresh shrimp for a small church luncheon. Her stomach rumbled, as she had not even had time to eat breakfast.

"Hello, Maggie."

It was strange how she sensed his presence behind her before he even spoke. She smiled as she turned around. "Why, hello, Miles Clinton Louis McAndrew the third."

"How are you?"

"Aside from wasting away from want of food, I am fine."

"Would you like some coffee?"

"Only if they come with beignets."

"It's a deal," he grinned.

Seconds later, they were situated at a table for two in a remote corner of Café du Monde. She sipped on her café au lait. "I am not a morning person."

He reached across the table and wiped away the sugar on her chin. "You look good in beignets."

She smiled wearily. "So where are you headed this fine

morning?"

"I was bringing my uncle's old civil war clothes to the new Memorial Hall. It took my aunt a year after his passing to go through his clothes, and since we heard that some confederates were opening this Hall, we decided to donate them."

"What a lovely gesture," she said.

"I'm surprised they let you out on your own."

"It was an emergency, and I guess Mother's beginning to trust me again." She couldn't help but think of their kisses and how her mother would react if she knew.

He leaned forward, quiet all of a sudden. His eyes grew serious. "I can't stop thinking about kissing you."

She blushed, not knowing what to say. She stirred her coffee with the spoon, watching the creamy liquid swirl. "Penelope would be so mad if she knew we were together right now."

"I really don't care what she would do. I am tired of her," he growled.

She looked fearfully at him. "What are you planning?"

"Well, I am certainly not going to marry her."

"Do you realize she's already told Darlene that you proposed?"

He sneered. "Of course, I do. She's insisting on a formal introduction to my family, and you know how well that would go over with Luci. I've stalled her as much as possible."

"What are you going to do?" she asked again.

"I haven't decided yet, but let me ask you this. Do you seriously think your mother would send you to a convent just for kissing me?"

She sighed. "I really don't know. Penelope would make it into something more than it was."

He crossed his arms and watched the people on the street as they started their day. "Damn it. I do not want to marry her. I don't love her. I love--" He stopped himself and glanced at Maggie. "What would it matter if your mother knew about the kiss if I asked you to marry me?"

He held up his hand. "And before you say anything, I have thought this through. I love you, Maggie, and despite the fact that Penelope has been around every time we're together, the only thing that has made it bearable is the fact that you were there as well."

Maggie stopped eating as the word *love* swirled in her head. She swallowed the beignet, taking a sip of coffee to wash it down. Then she met his eyes, and her heart sped up.

"How can you be so sure you love me?" she asked warily, unable to believe him.

He covered her hands with his and stared into her eyes. She felt he could see into her soul. He smiled crookedly.

"We're the same, you and I. We think alike." He tilted his head. "Sure, we have different interests, but what matters is that we share the same soul."

She nodded. "I know what you mean. There are times I've looked at you and known exactly what you were thinking."

They slipped into a comfortable silence, and she wondered if what she was feeling was true love. It felt different from the way she felt about Brent.

She suddenly jumped up, remembering the shrimp, her mother and the horse and carriage still waiting for her on the corner. "Oh, dear. I have to go."

He scooted his chair back and stood as well. "I do, too."

She headed toward the exit, stopped and gave him a questioning look. "Did you just propose to me?

He thought a second before replying. "I guess that depends on what your father will say."

* * * *

"Winston," Maggie said, surprised to see him in the parlor. She had thought she would be lunching with older, church ladies. Instead, the sight of her father sitting in his chair along with Penelope and her mother had her befuddled.

With a funny, fearful smile, she asked, "Where are the ladies from church, Mother?"

Winston had stood the moment she appeared and looked at her father. "May I?"

"Of course, son."

Her feet were rooted to the floor as Winston knelt at her feet. He held an open ring box out to her, and her heart fell into the pit of her stomach. She knew she was white as a sheet, and the last thing she heard before darkness overcame her was: "Will you be my wife?"

* * * *

The sharp odor of smelling salts brought Maggie out of her faint. She swiped at the hand holding it under her nose and blinked her eyes. She stared up into the face of her father. Her mother peered over his left shoulder, and Winston stood over his right. She was on the settee with a huge fat pillow under her head.

As her family gave her some room, she sat up slowly. Winston knelt once more and held out the ring. "I have very strong feelings for you, Maggie."

She stared at the huge sparkling diamond as if it were a black widow. "But, I don't love you."

"'Tis but a matter of time."

Her father's deep voice boomed through out the room, making her head pound. "I strongly urge you to accept."

"We can have a long engagement if you like," Winston pleaded.

"But, but you're thirty, and I'm only nineteen" Maggie whispered.

"Rebecca Jamison married a fifty year old, and she's not but eighteen," Penelope stated. Maggie refused to look at her, knowing she had something to do with this.

"Mother, please," she begged. "I...I love someone else."

Her mother crossed her arms. "And why has this man you love so much not called on you?"

Unwillingly, her eyes met Penelope's, and she shivered at the warning in her cousin's eyes. A cold smile became carved on her too-perfect face. "Uncle, while I was going to wait until Maggie's engagement was settled, I think I aught to warn you. Clinton will soon ask you for my hand in marriage."

Distractingly, Winston grabbed Maggie's hand and slipped the ring on her finger. "See how lovely it looks? I will buy you anything you want. My fortune will see our great, great, great grandchildren."

Maggie bit her lip, thinking of this morning's more appealing proposal. *Oh, Clint, why hadn't you beat him?*

As if thinking of him had conjured him, the butler announced his arrival. Clint appeared in the doorway with a determined look on his face. He searched the room, and as his eyes lit on the scene before him, his face fell. Maggie wanted to run to him and wipe away all doubts, but fate stepped in and took control. Or rather, Penelope did.

"Clinton, you're just in time to hear of Margarite's good news," Penelope sang.

"Yes, she has just accepted Winston's offer of marriage," her mother added, giving her a stern look.

And so, without even having to utter an affirmative answer, her family once again took charge, and it was assumed by all but one that she had agreed to be Winston's wife.

Chapter 12

June 27, 1891
Saturday

"Miss Margarite, there's a delivery for you at the back entrance," said the maid.

She looked from where she sat by the window. Her eyes were puffy and red, and she felt as if a huge rock sat on her chest. "Can't you accept it for me? I'm sure it's just more presents from Winston."

"The lad insisted he was to give it to you and you alone."

Dejectedly, she nodded. "Alright, then. I'll be down momentarily."

The maid left, and Maggie dried her eyes with a handkerchief. She splashed some water on her face and then went down. There was no one around when she entered the kitchen except the delivery boy. He sat at the table, hunched over a cup of coffee. His grey cap was pulled down over his face, and it wasn't until she cleared her throat that he cautiously looked up.

Her heart flipped at the sight of honey-brown eyes, and she nearly tripped on her skirts as she ran to his waiting arms. She bit her lip to keep from crying and buried her head in his chest. His hand ran soothingly up and down her back as he tried to calm her.

"Shhh, love, it's all right," Clint whispered.

"I don't love him," she cried.

He pulled back and looked at her tear-stained face. His lips thinned in anger. "Don't cry anymore. Please. We'll figure a way out."

"But, now you and Penelope…" Her eyes watered, and she looked away. "It's hopeless."

He glanced about to make sure they were still alone. "I never asked your father to marry her. He simply assumed that's why I was there."

"What difference does it make?" she whimpered. "I'm trapped. Father's already given him half of my dowry."

He kissed her then before she realized what he was doing. At first, she sank into it, forgetting everything but the world he instantly created for her. The second it ended, however, she stepped away, remembering where she was. She quickly checked to make sure no one had seen.

"God, Maggie," he growled.

Hearing the anger in his voice, she looked quizzically at him. "What? Why are you angry?"

"They've got you so much under their thumb, you're afraid to even breathe," he snarled.

She shook her head. "You don't know what I've been through."

"That's an excuse, Maggie. I'm sick of seeing you let them treat you like a slave. Maybe you should marry Winston. You can step right into another relationship with your father."

Her slap on his cheek stunned him momentarily. Then he smiled crookedly. "See, there is fire in there. You just haven't let it out yet."

He headed toward the door. "Let me know when you're

ready to be your own woman. Until then, I guess Penelope won't be such a bad wife after all."

* * * *

How dare he, Maggie thought, pacing in her room. *They don't rule me. I spent a year on my own. Well, not exactly on my own, but away from them, anyway, and I survived. I even learned a thing or two.*

She fought the urge to throw something, then reconsidered and a glass trinket shattered against the wall. It felt so good that she picked out several of Winston's presents and sent them flying through the air as well. By the time her mother swept into the room, her temper had cooled, and she was seated at the windowsill. Shocked, her mother stepped gingerly around all the glass.

"What on earth? Margarite, what is the meaning of this? Are these Winston's gifts?"

"Mostly."

Her mother crossed her arms and stood over her. "I believe an explanation is in order."

Thinking of Clint, she steeled her nerve and rose slowly to her feet. "I'm not marrying Winston."

"Oh, I beg to differ," her mother argued.

Narrowing her eyes, she held her ground. "Tell father he should get his money back, for I'll not be forced into a loveless marriage."

"But you accepted."

"No, you all assumed I accepted. Penelope's little...announcement foreshadowed Winston's proposal." She waved her hand in aggravation. "It doesn't matter anyway. I'm not marrying him."

The sparkling ring grabbed her attention, and she tugged it off. "Here. Better take this. I might accidentally smash it as well."

Her mother caught it just as she let it drop. "What has gotten into you, Margarite?"

She contemplated the question before quietly answering. "A pair of honey-brown eyes."

Her mother pursed her lips and crossed her arms. "Your secret admirer."

Maggie blushed and ducked her head. Then she forced herself to look her mother in the eyes. "Yes."

"Am I allowed to know his name?"

Maggie bit her lower lip. "I think it best if we wait."

Her mother let out a deep, weary sigh. She shook her head. "I just want someone to take care of you. Winston can do that."

Maggie smiled. "So can my admirer."

They studied each other for a moment. Then she held out her hand. "On second thought, I need Winston's ring back."

Her mother placed it in her hand. "Don't be rash."

"I'm following my heart, Mama. Why can't you understand?"

"Because the last time you followed your heart," her mother whispered. "You broke mine."

A single tear slid down the older woman's cheek, and Maggie threw her arms around her. It was the first real hug they'd had in over a year and a half. Soon, the two were sobbing in each other's arms. Their pain flowed and cleansed their souls, and when the storm had passed, they saw each other with brand new eyes.

Her mother cupped her face with her hands. "It must have been terrible for you."

Maggie shook her head. "No, no, it wasn't. Mrs. Belle and I got along perfectly. She's the cook. She took me under her wing and taught me a lot about cooking."

"I worried about you so much. I had trouble sleeping."

Maggie smiled sadly. "I was fine, Mama."

She stepped in front of her dressing table, picked up a clean cloth, and dipped it in water. Then she wiped her face and felt better for it. She ran a brush through her hair and then turned to her mother.

"I am going to give Winston his ring back."

Her mother nodded resignedly. "Have Donald take you."

Chapter 13

"I don't think you should go in there by yourself," the butler stated.

Maggie laid her hand on his arm. "I'll be fine, Donald. He is a gentleman, after all."

He shook his head. "Your mother'll skin me alive."

"She doesn't have to know."

She stepped away from the open-carriage and ascended the steps to Winston's rented house. They were only blocks from her parents' home, and yet she felt as if she were miles away. She took a deep breath, squared her shoulders and knocked on the front door.

Several knocks later, Winston finally answered. His clothes were in disarray, and he appeared to be half asleep. He squinted at her, and when she realized who she was, he became angry.

"Margarite, what are you doing here?" he barked. "S'not proper."

She wrung her hands. "May I come in? I have to speak with you."

Disgruntled, he looked up and down the street before holding the door open wide. The second she passed by him, he slammed the door shut. Startled, she jumped and looked at him as if he'd lost his mind. The anger on his face stopped her cold. Intimidated, she unconsciously took a step back, and like a lion stalking its prey, he stepped forward until he had her pinned against the wall.

Fear entered her heart as she wondered why he acted so strangely. Despite all the weeks they'd spent together, she really did not know him at all. He had always been the perfect gentleman, until now.

She grew uncomfortable under his silent and intent gaze. She opened her mouth to speak, but he chose that moment to kiss her for the first time ever. She gagged on the heavy taste of cherry syrup, and she lightly slapped his shoulder in an effort to get him to release her. He did, only to assault her cheek with his slimy tongue.

"Wanted to do that for a long time," he whispered. "And since we're betrothed…"

He swooped her into his arms and carried her towards the stairs leading to the second floor. She panicked and began to struggle. Her nails dug into his cheek, and he dropped her.

"Damn it, woman," he snarled.

"Stop, Winston, what is wrong with you?" she cried.

He ignored her question, grabbed her and threw her over his shoulder. Then he started up the stairs. Her hands reached out for anything that would stop them. Her fingertips slid over the wooden banister but couldn't get a good grip. She was afraid to struggle lest they tumble down the stairs. The combination of blood rushing to her head and the long view down made her dizzy. She closed her eyes and only opened them when she landed on a soft bed. She instantly tried to jump up, but he pushed her back down. He towered over her, and she scrambled to the head of the bed.

"Mr. Hampshire!"

Donald stood in the doorway. His big Irish body blocked it entirely. "What do you think you are doing?"

Quick as a snake, Winston reached under the mattress and pulled out a small handgun. He swung his arm around and fired a shot into the wall. The Irishman dove to the floor, and Winston aimed at his head.

"This don't concern you," he snarled. "Get the hell outta here."

The butler quickly did as he was told, and Winston turned to Maggie. He smiled drunkenly and waved the gun in the air.

"Works e'rytime," he laughed.

"Winston, are you drunk?" She tried to sound strong but had a feeling it came out as a whisper.

He shook his head. "Nope. Not a drinking man."

Wildly, she glanced about the room, and her eyes widened at the sight of his dresser. Empty cough syrup bottles were strewn all over it, and she noticed they were all over the floor as well. She looked at him in astonishment.

"Winston, you're an opium eater," she whispered.

"I am not," he yelled. His face grew dark with fury, and he descended upon her like a bull gone insane. "I have bronchitis."

He grabbed a fistful of her hair and pulled her close. "'Sides, isn't your place to question what I do."

He kissed her again and laid his body on top of hers. She was effectively pinned beneath him. She was doomed. Maggie panicked and fought, but was overpowered. His hands roamed her body like he owned it. Hot tears trailed down her face, and she did the only thing she knew to do. She screamed.

He clamped a hand over her mouth, and she bit him. His hand curled into a fist, and he raised it behind him. Then his weight was suddenly lifted off her. She sat up to see Clint beating the living daylights out of him. The man fought back and got in a few good licks before Donald jumped in and helped. He knocked Winston out with a good left hook.

"That's fer shooting at me," he yelled at the unconscious lump on the floor.

The bed dipped as Clint sat in front of her. His strong fingers gently curled around her shaky hands. He brought them to his lips and blew heat on them.

"You're cold."

Her mind was a blank. She tried to form words but found her teeth were chattering. A blanket was thrown over her shoulders, and she gave Donald a grateful glance. However, her eyes were quickly drawn back to Clint's comforting face. He was her port in the storm.

"Cough syrup," she managed to say at last. "W-Winston is an opium eater."

Shock spread over the features of Clint's face. Then he took notice of the bottles laying around the room. He picked up one from the nightstand that was half full.

"Ayers Cherry Pectoral," he read on the glass bottle. He picked up another and shook his head. "Graves' pectoral compound."

He handed it to Donald. "Did you know this one has ten grains of opium as well as twelve percent alcohol?"

"He said he had bronchitis," Maggie whispered.

Clint shook his head some more. "Maybe a long time ago. That's probably how he got started on this stuff."

She shuddered. "I want to go home."

"Where's Penelope?" Clint asked.

She shrugged. "I don't know."

His brows deepened. "Your mother thought she came with you."

Maggie tilted her head. "No, only with our butler."

"Well that was inappropriate," he scolded.

"I had to give him back his ring."

Suddenly remembering, she took the diamond off her finger and held it up for Clint to see. "Where should I leave this?"

Donald picked up a full bottle of pectoral. "We'll tie it to this and leave it on his bed."

She nodded and gave him the ring. Clint helped her up, and they started out of the room. Penelope's appearance in the doorway impeded their departure. Her cheery disposition changed to shock, and she hid the paper sack she held behind her back.

"What are ya'll doing here?" she asked cautiously.

"One could ask the same of you. What's in the bag?" Clint asked suspiciously.

"What, this? Just some cough syrup. Winston's a tad under the weather."

Donald snorted. "He is at that."

Penelope tried to peer into the room. "Where is he?"

"He's a tad on the floor," Clint stated matter-of-factly.

"What?" she cried and tried to push past them. Clint held her upper arms.

"Not a good idea, Pen," he advised. "He's already tried to take advantage of Maggie. No sense you giving him an opportunity."

Her eyes said it before the words came out of her mouth. "Too late."

Clint took a deep breath as a weight lifted off his shoulders. He held out his hand. "Good. Can I have my grandmother's ring back?"

Her shoulder sagged. She set the paper sack down and slipped the ring off. "It was too big anyway."

His fingers closed around the heirloom, but he wasn't through with her yet. "Please tell me he didn't involve you in his madness."

"I only get it for him," she growled through clenched teeth. "And what's so wrong with opium? Everybody does it."

His face held contempt. "Not respectable folks."

Anger marred her pretty features. "Winston is wealthy beyond imagination."

Clint held up his index finger. "I said respectable, not wealthy."

He grabbed Maggie's hand and pushed past Penelope. "Let's go, dear. I want a word with your father."

Chapter 14

"Mr. Lafitte," Clint began, "this ring was never intended for Penelope."

Maggie's hand was in Clint's death grip. The loveseat felt like it was stuffed with rocks, and the air in the house threatened to choke her. Her left eye twitched in an irritating manner, but she refused to let her nerves get the best of her again. She forced herself to breathe steady and evenly.

"What do you mean?" her father asked cautiously.

"That Sunday," Clint hesitated. "I came here to ask you for Maggie's hand, not Penelope's. Only, Winston beat me to the punch."

The elderly man drummed his fingers on the arm of the chair. "So what are you trying to say, young man?"

"I'm asking to take care of Maggie for the rest of her life. I love her deeply and want to be her husband."

There was a moment of complete silence as her father contemplated the request. "But what of my niece?"

"Penelope and I," Clint thought of how to address the situation. "We are not well suited, sir."

Her father looked at her. "And Winston?"

She chewed the tip of her little pinky. She did not want to go into details. "I returned his ring."

He grunted and got to his feet. He poured himself a

brandy, swallowed it down, and poured another. Then he reclaimed his seat and crossed his arms.

"You girls are going to be the death of me," he muttered. Then he extended his hand to Clint. "Welcome to the family, son, again."

As the two shook on it, Maggie let the affirmative answer sink in. Then she swiped at a tear that had snuck out and beamed with joy. She threw her arms around her father.

"Thank you, thank you, thank you," she gushed.

He looked at her in amazement. "If I had known you loved him... You should have come to me."

"But mother—"

"Pish on mother," he chided. He rubbed his belly. "Shall we celebrate with a nice dinner?"

* * * *

Maggie sat in the crook of Clint's arm. They were on the front porch watching the squirrels chase each other. Clint was lost in thought, and she poked his stomach.

"Too full for words?"

He sighed. "No, just thinking that Penelope gave up too easy and wondering why."

She nodded. "That had crossed my mind as well."

"You know something?"

"What?"

"I just realized that she hasn't been her usual demanding self."

Maggie frowned. "How so?"

"We've been too busy sneaking off to see that she's letting us."

"But why?"

The right corner of Clint's mouth lifted into a half smile. "She likes him."

Maggie grimaced and rolled her eyes. "Well, I guess so!

They have had relations."

"Who hasn't?"

She could tell by his expression that he hadn't meant for that to slip out. Her heart clenched in sudden apprehension and her throat went dry. She felt the blood drain from her cheeks.

"Please tell me you didn't," she whispered.

He hung his head. "I was young and stupid."

She let go of his hand. "When?"

He hesitated. "I guess about a year or so ago. One time only. From the way she hunted me afterwards, I guess she wanted more."

Maggie slapped his cheek soundly. "Miles Clinton McAndrew the third, how could you?"

His eyes darkened. "I didn't even know you then, Mags. Besides, weren't you paying your debt to society?"

Her pride stung from his minor reference to her infamous past. She stewed, trying to come up with a good retort but failing. She stood slowly.

"I believe I am tired. Good night, Mr. McAndrew."

He jumped to his feet and grabbed her arm. "No, we're not sleeping on this fight."

She shrugged. "It's not a fight."

He forced her to face him. Tenderly, his fingertips touched her chin and lifted until she looked at him. Honey swam in his eyes as they pleaded with her to understand.

"I did not chase her," he stated. "As you may recall, she blackmailed me."

"You mean she blackmailed me."

He frowned and shook his head. "Not just you, darling, she threatened to tell you about our little one night stand."

Her eyes ached with the need to shed tears. He pulled her to him before she could escape. "Let me seal my apology with a kiss."

"No," she whispered, but it was muffled against his soft lips.

She wanted to hate him. She wanted to hit him as well, but her body betrayed her. Maggie relaxed into his embrace as he explored her mouth. It ended all too soon when the front door slammed shut. They parted and waited for a tongue lashing.

"Have you two seen Penelope?" her mother asked worriedly.

"No," they replied in unison.

"I haven't seen her since this morning," her mother continued. "I'm worried. Clint, would you mind going to ask Mr. Hampshire if he's seen her?"

Maggie exchanged a look with him as he answered. "Yes, ma'am. I certainly will."

"I'm going, too," she stated.

"No," he growled.

"Yes, and that is that."

She grabbed his hand and dragged him down the steps. They stopped at the sound of her father's voice.

"Hold up," he ordered. "I think I need to go as well."

* * * *

Once again, Maggie chewed the tip of her pinky. She stood behind Clint, who stood behind her father as he knocked on Winston's door. When it was obvious that no response was forthcoming, her father tried the knob and boldly entered the open house. She had never seen her father move so quickly. He bypassed all the first floor rooms and went straight to the stairs.

"Where is his bedroom?" he asked gruffly.

Clint led the way then, and they were soon standing outside the closed bedroom door. Without hesitation, her father kicked it open. His face held a fury that she had rarely seen, and she actually felt sorry for her cousin.

The room, however, was empty, and they stood in an awkward silence. Ever keen with the eye, her father immediately inspected all the empty cough syrup bottles with his cane, as if he dared not have them touch his hands. He sighed and turned to the others with a weary face. Before he could speak, Penelope's laughter drifted through an open window. It was on the courtyard side, and her father hastened out of the room. Maggie and Clint were on his heels as he burst out of the back of the house.

"Penelope," her father bellowed.

Clint stopped instantly, and Maggie ran into him. She stepped around him to see, and she gasped in shock.

Penelope lay across a bench with one breast exposed to the world while Winston knelt at her side without his shirt. He was engrossed in playing with the aforementioned breast. Her head was thrown back, and her eyes were closed. In fact, her father had to say Penelope's name again, and even then, she was sluggish to respond.

"But she said she wasn't participating," Maggie whispered.

Clint gave her a dubious look before shrugging out of his jacket. Just as he stepped forward to cover Penelope, her father hit Winston with his cane and continued to do so until Clint finally managed to get it away from him. Then he had to physically restrain the older man from further attacking Winston.

"You son of a whoremonger," her father snarled as she took up Clinton's coat and handed it to an intoxicated Penelope.

Winston had scrambled to his feet and now hid behind the bench and Penelope. He held out his hand in an attempt to ward her father off.

"I assure you, sir, I had the best intentions."

Her father snorted. "I'll believe that when you show up to the wedding."

Winston gave him an indignant look. "I'm not marrying her. I'm marrying her."

His finger extended to Maggie, and she sneered at him. "Did you not get your ring off your bed?"

His brows furrowed, and he scratched his chin. "Yes, but I thought you lost it when we were kissing."

Her father shot her an incredulous glare, and Clint hurried to explain for her. "Not to worry, sir, Daniel and I stopped Winston before he could harm Maggie. Trust me, sir, she was an innocent to his advances."

Mr. Lafitte nodded and grabbed Penelope's arm. "As I said, Mr. Hampshire, I expect you at the house in the morning. I'll have a justice there to preside over the wedding."

* * * *

Maggie clung to Clint's hand as they watched a tearful Penelope beg with Maggie's father. She stood at the front door surrounded by her bags. She flung herself at his feet, and Maggie felt embarrassment for her. But there was nothing she could do to help her.

"Please, uncle, Winston will come for me. I just know he will."

"Penelope, we've waited all morning and all afternoon, and now it is time to go."

"My mother would hate you for this," she snarled.

He ignored her outburst. "The nuns will help you through this, Penelope. They can give you the guidance that I apparently cannot."

He then opened the door and carried her bags out, leaving her kneeling on the floor. Her face was tear-streaked, and her hair hung in disarray. Slowly, she got to her feet and gave Maggie a cold, heart-broken look.

"Find him, Margarite," she ordered. "Find him and tell him where I am. He'll come for me."

Clint shook his head. "It's no use, Penelope. He's gone. I saw for myself. His house is empty. He left you."

She bit her lip and stuck her nose in the air. "You're wrong. You'll see."

Then she turned on her heel and followed her uncle outside. Despite the fact that her cousin had been horrible to her, Maggie still felt sad for her. She remembered how it felt to be abandoned by a man who was supposed to have loved her. She shook off the memories and threw her arms around Clint. She buried her face in his chest and breathed in his cologne. As if sensing her distress, he wrapped his arms around her and kissed the top of her head.

"Have no fear, Mags," he whispered. "I promise to love you for the rest of my life."

ABOUT THE AUTHOR

Jo lives in Louisiana with her husband, Michael, and two sons. She's been writing stories since she was five, especially in high school. After her ten year high school reunion, she decided to get serious and pursue her dream of writing. She began scribbling words during lunch hours and breaks and will continue to do so as long as God favors her.

For your reading pleasure, we invite you to visit our web bookstore

WHISKEY CREEK PRESS

www.whiskeycreekpress.com